DEATH MAKES STRANGERS OF US ALL

Death Makes Strangers of Us All

by

R. B. Russell

Swan River Press
Dublin, Ireland
MMXXIV

Death Makes Strangers of Us All
by R. B. Russell

Published by
Swan River Press
at Æon House
Dublin, Ireland
June MMXXIV

www.swanriverpress.ie
brian@swanriverpress.ie

Cover design by Meggan Kehrli
from "Particular City" (2018)
by R. B. Russell

Set in Garamond by Ken Mackenzie

Paperback Edition
ISBN 978-1-78380-775-8

Swan River Press published
a limited hardback edition of
Death Makes Strangers of Us All
in February 2018.

Contents

Night Porter

Marianne had no choice but to take the position of night porter at the St. Denis Hotel; it was either that or have her job-seeker's allowance cut because she had already turned down too many other offers of work. She tried to tell herself that if she didn't think too much about the unsociable hours it really wasn't such a bad situation. Her shifts were from ten in the evening to seven in the morning, six days a week, and she reasoned that for several hours each day, especially those towards the end of her shift, she would be left alone to read; nobody would be looking over her shoulder.

Reading was what Marianne liked to do. Most of the jobs she had been offered would have reduced the time she could spend with her nose in a book (as her mother always said). Working as a night porter was a compromise she was willing to attempt, even if the manager, Mr. Lane, had been very uncertain about hiring a woman for the job. His fears appeared to be justified during her very first shift; at three in the morning a group of eight men, all drunk, tried to return to two rooms that had been booked for four people, and they became abusive when Marianne refused to let them all stay. She had been told by Mr. Lane to use her initiative, but she had also been warned not to do anything to put herself, or other guests, in danger. Marianne told the drunks that she would telephone for permission to let them in, but, instead, she called the police. As the local station was just around the corner in Dern Street the incident was cleared up surprisingly quickly. Quite where the men were taken away to didn't concern her; everything was in order once more.

On her second night Marianne booked an elderly couple into a double room just after midnight, only to have the woman appear an hour later to report that her husband had died. It was a heart attack, apparently, and entirely natural, but it still shook Marianne.

And on her third night working at the St. Denis, a guest set light to their bedding at two in the morning. More damage was caused by the fire brigade than by the fire itself, and evacuating the other guests caused chaos. Marianne stayed on after her shift to help to clean up, and for the following week there seemed to be no end to the work required to set everything straight again. She had to admit to herself that she had certain obsessive-compulsive tendencies; she hated disorganisation and mess.

Marianne couldn't help wondering what might happen next, having called out the emergency services three times in her first three nights, but after those incidents everything seemed to go quiet. For the following few weeks the guests were all well-behaved and there were no dramas. A number of odd characters passed through the hotel, but after a while she failed to notice or even remember the more eccentric guests; they became simply names that she would enter into the register, faces she would never see again. The job was a compromise, but one that she could live with because every night she managed to find several uninterrupted hours to read. The only time she had to put her book down was when, once an hour, she was expected to walk up and down the corridors, on the three floors, just to make sure that everything was in order. She dutifully padded around the small hotel seeing nothing untoward, and hearing, at worst, the muted sounds of sexual activity, loud snoring, or the television playing quietly in the room of an insomniac. She would return to the book she had left at the front desk, and would continue to read, undisturbed, for another fifty-five minutes, until she would have to walk around the corridors once again.

And then, two months into her job, at about half past one in the morning, while she was reading a Ruth Rendell novel, a large and expensive silver Mercedes pulled into the small car park in front of the hotel. A woman got out of the front of the vehicle and helped a young man from one of the back doors. She almost carried him across the car park and into the reception.

"A room for the night," said the woman who was rather too-well presented in her sharply-pressed grey trouser suit, and too perfectly groomed for that time of the morning. Marianne had noticed that all of their usual guests would look rather uncared-for by the early hours.

"Just the one bed," the woman added. "My friend is rather tired and a little emotional. He won't be able to go home until the morning."

"Don't you think he ought to go to a hospital?" asked Marianne. There was nothing obviously wrong with him, but he appeared to be confused. He was not necessarily drunk, but it struck Marianne that he might be on drugs. He also looked a great deal younger than her companion, which seemed odd. His "supporter" had to be in her fifties, if not older.

"No, he's fine," said the woman. "Nothing that a decent night's sleep won't cure. How much is a room?"

"Sixty pounds, with breakfast."

"I really do just want to go to bed," said the young man suddenly. "I feel a little wobbly on my feet."

"Look, here's a nice round hundred pounds in cash," said the woman. "I'll happily pay the extra because there's a chance he might sleep-in tomorrow and I don't want any fuss if he does. He'll miss breakfast, I'm sure, but he's bound to wake up and clear out before anyone needs to clean the room."

Marianne wanted to say no, sensing trouble, but didn't feel confident enough to turn them away.

"Is there a problem?" asked the woman.

"No, that will be fine," replied Marianne, deciding that the risk was worth taking. However, she insisted on seeing identification for the guest, and from the woman who was paying.

Marianne told Miss Fisher that she could take Mr. Charles up to 34. It was the room that Mr. Lane said should be used by guests who looked likely to make any kind of disturbance. It was the only bedroom in the hotel without any immediate neighbours, and was one of the few that had not been recently refurbished. The young man was helped up the stairs by his unlikely companion, and Marianne resolved that she would give them only a couple of minutes before going to check that nothing untoward was taking place. In her mind she uncomfortably played out scenarios involving Rohypnol and rape, but just as she was about to go up, Miss Fisher came back downstairs. Marianne was assured that Mr. Charles was fine, and the woman left.

Marianne returned to her Ruth Rendell novel, but found it hard to concentrate. She wondered whether she hadn't read too much modern detective fiction. Miss Fisher and her friend had worried Marianne, but she couldn't really explain why. She remembered that the extra £40 in the till needed to be either accounted for or taken as a tip, and in the end she decided to have it for herself. She had earned it in those two minutes when she had worried what might be happening in Room 34.

The incident of the "tired and emotional" guest and her "friend" vaguely troubled Marianne all day. When she arrived at work the following evening, she asked the manager:

"Was everything alright after last night?"

"Fine. Any reason it shouldn't be?"

"A young man was brought in by a friend and he seemed the worse for wear . . . I nearly said 'no', but in the end I put him in Room 34."

"I've not heard of any problems."

And so began an ordinary, uneventful evening. Marianne was steadily busy until one o'clock but there had been nothing demanding to attend to; in between guests coming and going she had tidied up the reception area and the office. Once it was quiet she returned to her Ruth Rendell paperback and the rest of her shift slipped by without her really noticing it.

Marianne had the following night off work. She kept to her usual routine, going to bed at seven in the morning, and getting up again at two in the afternoon. Over the past few months she had become increasingly frustrated by living with her mother, and had considered moving out. She was finally earning some money and could probably pay rent for a room somewhere, or even a small flat. However, now that her hours didn't coincide so frequently with her mother's, she was more content with the present arrangement.

She read during the afternoon, and went out just before her mother returned from work. Marianne had an hour to browse in a local bookshop before it closed, and finding a Henning Mankell paperback she hadn't read before, she decided to treat herself to dinner in a local pub. A regular wage was still a novelty, and it felt wrong to pay for a meal when her mother would have been happy to cook for her. However, it felt good to be out, and she started to read her book as she waited for her food, and then as she ate.

Marianne was interrupted just as she was finishing her meal; some old school-friends had arrived to celebrate a birthday, and she stayed drinking with them until after closing time. Before she had taken her job as night porter she would have declined the invitation to go on to a club, but she was still wide awake, and they spent the rest of the evening in the Milky Way on Mill Street. Marianne would have liked to have found somebody to take home, and once again regretted not having a place of her own. However, relationships were going to be even harder to find now that she kept the hours she did.

At work the next night it was very quiet, with very few guests booked into the hotel, and all of them back quietly in their rooms by eleven, which was how Marianne liked it. She tidied up the reception area and wiped down the tables and the insides of the windows. It had turned cold and there were occasional snow-flurries outside, which seemed to keep people off the streets. When everything was tidy, Marianne sat at the counter and continued reading her Henning Mankell paperback.

She had walked the corridors twice that evening, and was back at the reception desk with her book when she happened to look up, and stare out of the glazed front door. She was wondering whether the settled snow really amounted to even a centimetre, when the Mercedes drove into the car park. She recognised it as the expensive silver model that had brought Mr. Charles as an overnight guest only the week before. Once again, the older woman got out of the driving seat and helped somebody else out of the car. As happened the previous week, she had to support this second person as they made their way to the front door.

"Miss Fisher," said Marianne in her most neutral, professional voice.

"Good evening. You were on the desk last week, weren't you?"

"Yes, when you paid for a room for Mr. Charles."

"That's right, and I can't believe that I'm in a similar situation tonight . . . My friend's name is Fitzpatrick. He's had a very, very long day. I made the same mistake as with Mr. Charles of taking him out to a restaurant rather than bringing him straight here . . . He really will be no trouble."

"I would rather not book him in, not in this state."

"But you let my other friend stay."

"I did, but I shouldn't have done."

"Was he any trouble?"

"No."

"Well, then. Mr. Fitzpatrick is just the same; tired and a little drunk."

Marianne could not make up her mind what to do. During her job interview Mr. Lane had put various awkward scenarios before Marianne and he had obviously been pleased by her common-sense replies. This wasn't as clear-cut a situation as any she had been asked about, though, and she hesitated.

Miss Fisher had to prompt her again for a decision.

"Room 34 is available," Marianne agreed reluctantly. "That will be £60. I will need to see identification, as before."

"Of course."

Miss Fisher smiled, but Marianne did not feel able to trust the woman. She recognised her own prejudice against this self-confident older woman, with her heavy make-up and expensive clothes. And she hated herself for agreeing to do as the woman asked. While Miss Fisher took Mr. Fitzpatrick up to his room, Marianne went to put the cash in the till and found that she had, again, been paid £100 in notes. This time she put the difference into the charity box.

As before, Miss Fisher was back down again in less than a couple of minutes. Once the Mercedes had driven away Marianne went upstairs and stood outside the door of Number 34, listening, but she could not hear a sound. The young man was probably asleep, or trying to get to sleep, but this time Marianne knocked. She had decided that she would have to be honest and say that she was concerned; worried because he had looked so ill. It might get her into trouble, disturbing a guest, but her conscience insisted that she had to take the risk.

There was no answer. Marianne knocked once more. It was still strangely quiet, so she went down to the office and make a new electronic card key. After knocking again at the door of Room 34 and still receiving no reply, she unlocked it and walked inside.

Marianne was immediately hit by an icy cold. Her first thought was that Fisher had left the window open to help the young man sober up, but in the streetlight that flooded into the room Marianne could see the window was closed. The room was empty. Nor was Fitzpatrick in the *en suite* bathroom.

Marianne checked the window, wondering if the young man had climbed out of it, but it was firmly locked from the inside. Anyway, there was quite a drop to the street below, and down on the pavement there were no footprints in the snow.

Fitzpatrick couldn't have passed Marianne on the stairs, and the lift hadn't been used. The disconcerted night porter went back down and looked at the security tapes in the office. They showed that the young man had not come back through the lobby at any time; he had simply disappeared.

She couldn't decide what to do. She considered calling the police, but where was the evidence of foul-play? The guest was free to leave whenever and however he chose to, and the fact that she had not seen him go could always have been her mistake.

While she tried to decide what to do, Marianne made sure that her note of the name and address of Miss Stephanie Fisher was recorded legibly, and as an after-thought she made a separate note for herself. She told herself that she was being unreasonably over-careful, but in the office she played back the digital recording from the security camera in the car park and took down the registration number of the silver Mercedes. Just to be sure, she copied the file containing the footage from the front desk camera into a new folder on the computer; she did not want it to be erased after a couple of days.

Marianne found it impossible to get back to her Henning Mankell book. It suddenly grated on her that the novel was set in Sweden during a heat-wave, while in Britain it was snowing. She was also annoyed to discover that she had previously been reading the Mankell books "out of sequence". But the cause of her discontentment wasn't really the book.

"I don't know," said Mr. Lane simply. "I asked the cleaner and she doesn't remember having had to do anything in Room 34 for weeks. To be honest, I'm not going to worry. Your Miss Fisher has paid the bills and nobody's done anything wrong. Although we can't think of an explanation for a disappearing guest, that doesn't mean there isn't one."

"If she comes in again, wanting a room for another young man, I'll refuse to book them in. And I'll call the police."

"If you really think there's something illegal going on, by all means tell them to try another hotel."

And that is exactly what Marianne suggested when Miss Fisher arrived the following week. Once more it was a young man she brought with her. They had all been the same kind of pretty-boy that annoyed her; she preferred her men a little more, well, masculine. They had all been under the influence of drink or drugs, and Marianne had read enough crime novels to be able to imagine all manner of reasons for Fisher dumping them at the hotel. They could well have been robbed or abused. Prostitution was possible. The only part of the whole story that Marianne did not understand was how the previous guest had managed to disappear from his room, and why.

"Which hotel do you suggest?" Miss Fisher asked, pleasantly enough.

It was three in the morning and, although it wasn't snowing this time, it was bitterly cold outside. The man was even younger than the previous two, perhaps even younger than Marianne herself. She was uncomfortable when she realised that she actually felt something maternal or protective towards him, and Marianne asked herself if turning him away was the best thing for his safety. If she booked him in, then at least she would make sure that this time she kept a close eye on him. She would put him into a different room from where the only other way out would be through a window into an inner courtyard.

"Room 18," she said. "I'll have to come up with you."

"There really is no need," said Fisher. "I can take Mr. Evans up to his room."

"I need to re-set the lock on the door," Marianne lied. "It will only take a second."

All three of them went up to the room with Marianne leading the way. She opened the door with her master key-card and explained, as nonchalantly as she could, that it would now be reset. She then made sure that Fisher's key worked and she handed it over to her. The woman took the young man inside and Marianne used her master key to go into the room opposite, which she knew to be empty.

She watched through the squint in the door, and when Fisher left Marianne waited for her to walk down the corridor before she came out. She listened to the woman going down the stairs, and although she couldn't hear the woman crossing the hall past the unmanned reception desk, she felt the slight change in pressure as the front door opened and closed.

Marianne risked getting into a great deal of trouble, but, nevertheless, she opened the door to Room 18 with her master key and walked in.

"Please excuse me," she said, immediately noticing how cold it was in the darkened room. "I do apologise, but I . . . "

Her first reaction had been to look towards the window again, to see if it was open, which it wasn't. But her attention was immediately taken by the young man standing just inside the brightly-lit bathroom. He was wearing only a tee-shirt and his hands were tied to the door handle with what looked like a dirty strip of some white material. He was obviously distressed; he was gagged and the look in his eyes was at first wild, but then suddenly hopeful, pleading. Then he looked from Marianne to somebody else who was inside the bathroom with him.

Suddenly that person pushed past the terrified young man. The first thing that struck Marianne was that the man who appeared was really very, very old. He had a long face and his wrinkles were deep, like the cracks in dried earth. He was also completely bald. He was dressed in a brown suit that, even back-lit from the bathroom and almost entirely in silhouette, appeared dirty and stained. In one hand he carried a hotel towel, and in the other he had a huge hypodermic syringe that looked like it was made of corroded brass.

"You shouldn't be here," he said with a low, quiet but insistent voice.

"I'm the night porter," said Marianne, without thinking.

"I know, night porter," the man said. "Can we agree that you have seen nothing here? Would you like to leave and never think about this again? It would be for the best."

Marianne reasoned that she could be out of the room and downstairs, phoning for the police, long before the old man caught up with her. But the young man was staring at her, trying to scream at her to stay and help him.

"No," said Marianne, shaking, still considering running. "*You* can leave."

"I will, when I've finished."

And the man was across the room with an unbelievable speed and agility. Instinctively Marianne flung the door open to run out and it crashed into him.

That should have given Marianne enough time, but as she reached the stairs she could already hear the man coming down the corridor towards her. Marianne vaulted over the bannisters between the two sections of the dog-leg stair and managed to get her footing right as she landed. She took another leap into the reception area and ran across to the desk. She immediately picked up the telephone and hit nine three times before looking up.

The man was already standing by her as they both heard the distant, tiny voice asking which emergency service was required.

"Police," said Marianne, upset by how shaky and thin her voice sounded. How had the man appeared so quickly beside her? What did he intend to do with the syringe he was holding?

But the old man just smiled at Marianne, and walked away, backwards. Although he appeared quite calm, and the movement was effortless, the man seemed to move too quick; he was at the stairs and climbing them backwards, too soon, before he should have done . . .

"The St. Denis Hotel," Marianne added into the mouthpiece of the phone. "A guest is in danger, Room 18 . . . "

She put the receiver down on the counter and unwillingly returned to the foot of the stairs. She looked up, but the old man was gone; he would already be in the corridor. Marianne followed reluctantly, and when she saw that the first floor corridor was empty, she made herself walk along to the door of Room 18.

She hesitated before going back inside, but Room 18 was now empty; both the old man and the young man had gone. It took a great deal of courage for Marianne to look around the door into the bathroom, and she wasn't sure if she really felt any relief in finding nobody there. The only signs that there had ever been anybody in Room 18 were the horrible piece of material still attached to the door handle, the towel on the floor, and the state of the sink. There were dark marks on the white porcelain, as though somebody had been washing something very black and oily in it.

The police took seriously the call from Marianne. The security tapes clearly showed Miss Fisher and the young Mr. Evans, leaving the silver Mercedes and entering the hotel lobby. Fisher was traced through the number plate and questioned, but Marianne was told that she could have had nothing to do with the disappearance of Evans. Traffic cameras clearly showed her driving away as soon as she had left the hotel. Evans had apparently been acting as Miss Fisher's "escort" that night, quite legitimately.

The old man with the bald head didn't appear on the security tapes at all. There was only a partial shot of Marianne herself at the telephone calling the police; unfortunately, the cameras were angled too far towards the front door to show the whole reception desk.

Marianne was given a couple of weeks off work, paid, by Mr. Lane. It was very good of him, thought Marianne, who felt bad taking the money when she didn't intend going back. How could she return after what had happened? The idea of being alone in the hotel at night was unimaginable. Well, not quite alone; there would be guests, of course, locked away in their rooms. But who else might be behind the closed bedroom doors? The old, bald man?

Marianne continued to keep the hours that she had done when working at the St. Denis. She didn't admit to her mother that anything had happened at the hotel; instead she would go to the Milky Way until five in the morning, and then walk around the streets, sobering-up in the cold dawn until she could go home after seven. She would still go to bed at the same time, although she would now be getting up at more like four in the afternoon.

Not that she could sleep; Miss Fisher and the old man insisted on invading her thoughts as she lay awake in bed, threatening to enter her dreams if she dared to lose consciousness.

Marianne had never been a regular anywhere before, but the Milky Way made it easy for her. She knew one of the barmen who worked there during the week, and at the weekends her old school-friends would turn up. It was dark and full of alcoves where she could hide away and nurse a drink for hours if she had to. However, she soon got to know several other regulars, including a middle-aged man called Anthony, who she was becoming quite attached to. Anthony was an insomniac, and, distressingly, probably an alcoholic. Marianne worried that she might end up the same as him, but she enjoyed his company, and he seemed to tolerate hers. Marianne knew that she could not keep up the lifestyle indefinitely, not least because the St. Denis Hotel stopped her pay after two weeks, and the little money she had saved was already dwindling. She was convinced that her mother would find out what had happened, as Mr. Lane telephoned every week to ask after Marianne, leaving messages on the answer-phone. (Luckily, Marianne had always managed to intercept and erase them.) The hotel manager was trying to make it easy for her, Marianne knew that. She also knew that at some point she would have to re-apply to the benefits agency, and Lane could easily tell them that she had just walked out of the job. Then there wouldn't be any money coming in for at least a month.

It was three weeks later, perhaps four (Marianne had lost some sense of time), when she saw Miss Fisher walk into the Milky Way. It was a weeknight, and not at all crowded. Having bought drinks at the bar, Fisher sat at a table at the back. With her was yet another young man.

Marianne had been talking to Anthony. At some point in their friendship she had told him about the hotel and Fisher. She now pointed the woman out to him.

"Ask her," he said, and because Marianne had finished her fourth glass of wine, and felt safe in such a public place, she did so.

"The police have already interviewed me," Fisher insisted, uncomfortable at having Marianne confronting her across the table.

"I know, and they could *prove* nothing," said Marianne.

"Because there's nothing to prove! You gave them a description of the man they need to talk to."

"It's too much of a coincidence," Marianne dismissed the reply. "You're in league with the bald old man."

"I really don't know him. Look, I'm here for a quiet drink with my friend . . . "

"Another one of your escorts?" She turned to the young man, who looked confused at the sudden appearance of Marianne and her accusations.

"I hope she's paying you well?" Marianne asked. "I don't know what services she'll ask of you, but if she tries taking you back to a hotel afterwards, don't let her. There'll be an old man with a rusty hypodermic waiting for you."

"Please, Miss . . . Night Porter," said Fisher. "Please leave us alone. Otherwise I'll have to call the management."

"And tell them what? I'm a regular here, don't you know?"

"I like to have company of an evening. I'll take a companion to a restaurant, or a bar, or sometimes a club like this. When my young friend is tired I drop him off at a hotel with a couple of hundred pounds in his pocket to thank him."

"And that's when they meet your bald friend . . . "

The young man had been looking increasingly uncomfortable, and Marianne watched in amusement as Fisher opened up her purse, handed him some notes, and told him that he could go.

"I hope you're feeling happy with yourself," said Fisher, as the young man walked away.

"If I've saved his life, yes!"

"And how, exactly, have you done that?"

"By saving him from you, and the old man who disposes of your 'escorts' for you."

"And how does he dispose of them?"

"I don't know," said Marianne. "Perhaps he injects them with something to dissolve them . . . so all that's left is an oily, fatty mess in the sink!"

Fisher laughed, to which Marianne took exception. She hadn't realised how drunk she was, or how tired. She realised that she had voiced a private fantasy that really was too fanciful. She decided to leave Fisher and the scene of her

22

minor triumph, resolving to walk away without looking back. She made her way back to Anthony and apologised to him, saying that she was going home. She was depressed that he simply said goodnight and let her go. She looked back at him on her way out, and he was heading for the bar.

As she was leaving, Marianne went in to the "ladies". She sat on the toilet and replayed the scene with Fisher in her head, confused, unable to decide if she had made any sense. As Marianne walked out of the cubicle she heard the main door open and Miss Fisher walked in.

"I have nothing to hide, night porter," said the woman.

"You drug your young victims," said Marianne, wondering why she was continuing to be confrontational when all she wanted to do was leave.

"No, I don't drug them. I buy them a decent meal and they usually end up drinking too much."

"It's called prostitution."

"No, they only act as company. Nothing sexual happens."

"No?" asked Marianne. She was relieved to have been able to get past the woman, and was now close to the door, able to leave.

"Night porter, how I envy you," said Fisher. "And the young men I pay to keep me company. I admire your youth, your vitality, your innocence . . . "

"Bullshit."

"You could help me meet young men. There would be something in it for you . . . "

Fisher had come forward, almost without Marianne noticing. She pushed the older woman back and she stumbled, then slipped on the wet floor. There was a horrible sound as her head hit the dirty cracked tiles.

The woman didn't move. And Marianne didn't have time to see if she was dead or just unconscious because a blast of cold air accompanied the sound of another cubicle door opening. She had thought they were alone, and she was confused to see that it was the cubicle she had, herself, just come out of.

Suddenly there was the old, bald man with the deep wrinkles. He looked at Marianne, then at Miss Fisher, and he smiled.

"I'll finish her off for you," he said. "In a few moments there will be nothing."

"I don't want to know," said Marianne, backing away.

"Good, good. Then we can agree that you have seen nothing here. Leave and never think about this again."

"But why help me?" asked Marianne, although her voice was so quiet she hardly knew whether she had articulated her thoughts.

"Why?" asked the old man. "I was always there to tidy up for you before. And I'll be there when you need me again."

At the End of the World

I was disappointed to discover that my brother, Paul, when he finally came back from his adventures in South America, decided to take up residence in one of the old converted railway carriages on Pagham beach. It was the last place I would have expected him to want to live. These unlikely dwellings were originally Victorian coaching stock that had previously been owned by the London and Brighton South Coast Railway. In the 1920s the company stripped down the carriages to their wooden carcasses, they then sold them off to individuals who set them up on sleepers on the shingle. In this way Pagham became an unlikely and isolated inter-war shanty town.

Paul and I knew the place because our family holidayed there in the 1970s, staying at the local caravan park on the other side of the lagoon. Paul would tell anyone who listened just how much he hated the place. He railed against the caravaners from London and Essex, and the lonely and anti-social bird-watchers who would stand around the featureless lagoon with their binoculars and notebooks (the only people, Paul said, who visited Pagham out of choice). If we had ever seen them, he would also have complained about the elderly residents of the railway carriages. By then, most of the old coaches had been converted into miserable, squat bungalows with mostly invisible inhabitants. A few carriages remained unmolested, however, often decaying, set amongst thickets of stunted trees and brambles on the edge of the beach, and I remember being intrigued by these survivals. I don't know what Paul thought of them; he was not inclined to find anything interesting about the place.

I remember my brother moaning about the nasty little penny arcade, the insanitary café, and the mean shops selling plastic buckets and spades, but it was Pagham beach itself that he hated more than anything. He once claimed that the view over the shingle would have gone on forever, monotonously, if only it could have been bothered. We were standing on the beach in such a position that the shingle met the sky and there was nothing intervening . . .

"You do realise," he said. "This is the end of the world. There's nothing beyond this."

Paul's horror of the beach infected me. I disliked the effort of walking over the shingle, and I loathed the perpetual stink of seaweed, salt, and decaying fish. I also despised the way the sea kale and the thorn bushes pushed up through the shingle and attracted the bleached detritus that washed up from the boats out on the English Channel.

I know that Paul's attitude had a great influence over me. He was seven years older and I was in awe of his apparent sophistication. I understand now how desperately he needed to escape home and experience the world, which is just what he did as soon as he could. After school he refused to go to university and moved to Paris instead. My parents despaired of him; almost immediately he was in trouble with the authorities, and he went to prison for six months for taking part in a violent demonstration that made international news. Of all places, I recall that our family were in a caravan at Pagham when we heard that Paul had been arrested. My father came back from queuing for an hour at the public payphone, having had to make expensive international calls with a large pile of ten pence pieces, and he was furious. I think he was thoroughly ashamed, too; he had been forced to shout into the phone to make himself heard, and everyone in the queue knew what had happened.

After prison, my brother went to Germany and something bad happened there that meant he had to leave in a hurry. He got into the USA, somehow. He was in and around New York for some years, getting into more trouble until, finally, he had to relocate to Mexico. As I was a teenager he was a romantic hero to me. I didn't see him often, but he kept in touch by postcard and aerogram (which I kept in an album, cross-referenced with pages from an old school atlas to highlight exactly where he was in the world). I think Paul came home to stay with us only twice in ten years. He had different, glamorous, and feisty girlfriends with him, and he spent the whole time talking of revolution. When I left school and started work in local government I expected Paul to be horrified, but he simply sent me an obscene postcard with a note on the back wishing me well in my new job.

For many years he had been living in Cuba, despite an uneasy relationship with the authorities. But then, unexpectedly, two years ago he moved back to the UK and bought one of the converted railway carriages on Pagham beach. I don't know where he got the money from, or how he lived or paid his bills. I didn't ask when I finally found the courage to visit him last summer.

I was nervous of seeing Paul again, but, surprisingly, I had a thoroughly relaxing holiday. My job had been very stressful for some time: I had become involved in local politics and was trying to disassociate myself from a controversial planning decision which was always going to cause trouble. I needed to escape, and it was wonderful to be able to sit in the sun in front of Paul's old railway carriage, reading randomly from his eclectic collection of paperbacks, drinking bad coffee in the mornings, and cheap wine through the afternoons and into the evenings. The view over the shingle was dull and didn't quite include the sea, but that was not a problem; drunken tedium was a kind of balm at that time. Most evenings we walked down Lagoon Road and propped up the bar at the Spartan local hotel, before dragging ourselves back home, long after closing time. Somehow we managed to talk a great deal, but discussed nothing. Our lives were so different that we might have learnt a lot from each other, but equally, we could have ended up arguing. Paul's opinions and beliefs were basically anarchist and he could be quite dogmatic, but he was also an "inclusionist", as he called himself. He was genuinely happy to embrace people with different ideas to his own. I like to think that he also appreciated the permanency of our blood relationship. He seemed not to want to endanger that, and I appreciated the effort he made to make me feel welcome.

I visited Paul at Pagham for the second time last January, unexpectedly. I could not announce my arrival; he had no landline or even a mobile phone. I had gone to Portsmouth for a conference and planned to drive back to Cambridge on the Friday afternoon. The final session had dragged on, and the Friday rush-hour traffic had started early. The radio gave warnings of a serious accident on the motorway stretch of the A3, and the rain was coming down with determination. Spending the night with Paul seemed to be the sensible alternative to hours and hours on the road.

I arrived at Pagham at four in the afternoon and it was already dark. The few cars that I saw all had their lights on. Sea Lane is a singularly soulless road; too wide, with the bungalows set back from it. There were no people to be seen, and if it weren't for occasional lights in distant windows I'd have thought the place deserted.

At the despondent little roundabout the fish-and-chip shop was open, desperately trying to attract custom by pouring a horrible, sickly, lemon-yellow light out into the gloom. At the convenience store opposite, tired and faded bunting was flapping around a wire trolley filled with plastic buckets and rubber rings.

I was suddenly horrified by the thought that Paul might not be at home. I could not possibly stay in Pagham for the night alone! But the idea that I might have to find my way back up to the A27 filled me with despair. I drove down Lagoon Road with care, knowing that the standing water was hiding treacherous pot-holes, and praying that my journey wasn't in vain. Once again the converted carriages and ad hoc fences between them reminded me of a shanty-town. The place would have been called a *favela* or a *barrio* if it had been in South America. It looked even more eerie and impermanent in the half-light of that stormy evening.

There was a gap of a hundred yards or so after the last bungalow before a clump of stunted trees. Paul's place could be found parallel to the last remnants of the unmaintained road. To my great relief there was a faint light showing through the series of four small windows set into the side of the carriage.

I parked as close as I could and ran to the door. In the wind, the rain was coming at me horizontally and I was soaked through my coat by the time Paul answered.

"You want to stay the night?" he asked, as though he thought it was a ludicrous idea. We were standing just inside the front door.

"I can't face the drive back home."

As he looked so unwelcoming I added, "I can leave first thing in the morning."

"No, no, you can stay, of course. I'd never turn you away. But there's going to be a fair old storm tonight, and this is the last place on earth you want to be when the weather's foul."

"Far better than sitting in traffic on a motorway . . . I can go and find an off licence and buy some wine. If you bank up the fire we can get drunk and it'll be cosy."

"In January it's never cosy here; it's just cold. You won't believe how cold . . . The best bet is to go to bed as early as you can, and hope for better conditions in the morning."

"If you like, that's fine by me. I've had a very tiring few days in a conference centre."

"You really want to stay?"

I nodded. I still hadn't taken my coat off.

"Okay," he conceded, "but it may be dangerous." He said it quite matter-of-factly. He'd been drinking, but he appeared to be completely serious.

"How can it be dangerous?"

"I attract trouble; you know that."

When I said I didn't understand he took my coat and we went through to his living room. It was badly-lit, which was fine because it disguised the fact that the place was a mess and not particularly clean. It was also badly heated, although Paul did turn up the paraffin stove. He went into the kitchen and put on the kettle, shouting back that he assumed I would want something for dinner that evening. When I shouted that he was right, he came in and offered bacon sandwiches.

Despite the initial lack of welcome, we had a jolly few hours, eating, drinking Paul's strong tea, and listening to The Rolling Stones on an old stereogram at high volume. I guessed that Paul had been drinking wine on his own, but he didn't return to it until around eight. I offered, again, to go and buy some wine, although the weather was getting worse still, and I really didn't want to go back outside. I could hear the rain being hurled against not just the windows, but also the wooden walls and the tarred roof.

"No need; I've more wine," said my brother, who poured very generous measures once he had found another glass for me.

"It's getting even wilder out there," I said.

"You don't know the half of it. But then . . . "

He shrugged. He seemed to be distracted, disconcerted even, as though waiting for something, or someone. When I pressed him to explain he said, "You know, all my life I've been up for a fight. I don't know whether I've been looking for trouble, or whether trouble has followed me . . . perhaps it's come looking for me . . .

"I left home wanting adventure . . . and to escape a drug dealer I owed money to. In Paris I joined a lot of students in a protest, knowing it would get violent. I decided I was a Marxist. Actually, I still am, only I'm not as desperate as I was then to convert the rest of the world by force. I actually ran up to the riot police and dared them to hit me. And then some stupid *gendarme* put down his shield and tried to reason with me. That's when I punched him.

"In Berlin, I lived in a squat with a bunch of anarchists, and met a girl called Magda. She was in love with an idiot who fancied himself as the leader of a new Baader-Meinhof-style gang, and I decided I could be more radical than him. I did some things that were incredibly stupid. Finally, I stole a load of explosives from a British Army base, and hid them under my bed. Magda thought it was cool to make love on top of a haul of TNT. And then, one day, when I happened to be out, it all blew up, with Magda, and the idiot, and the rest of the anarchists. The police couldn't prove I had anything to do with it. There was no house. It blew up half the street. So I left for the USA.

"I was even more angry and confused than when I'd left home for Paris. I'd killed the girl I thought I loved, and my few other friends in the world. I got into the United States illegally, of course. They wouldn't have let me in if I'd asked them, not with my record. I got into all kinds of trouble, met a girl called Allyson who died of an overdose, went to live in the wilds of Manitoba, got involved in a car ring and a drugs syndicate, then went to New York and got mixed up in all kinds of other shit . . . "

He dismissed a couple of decades of his life with a wave of his hand, and started to talk about Mexico. He claimed to have lived well and made money, but he was always in danger, and found Cuba a safe haven.

All the time he had been talking the wind had become so furious that it sounded as though it was hurling shingle at the railway carriage rather than rain. As Paul related his story his voice became louder and louder so that he could make himself heard over the tempest. Rain had started to leak through the ceiling by the door and he had put an aluminium pan under the drip. Somehow, the sound of the water falling into the pan insistently repeated at a volume out of all proportion to the size of drops.

And then, as Paul talked about Cuba, the carriage seemed briefly to lift on one side, before falling back on its rotten sleepers.

"I did things for the authorities that they never officially sanctioned," he said. "I travelled to and fro on a succession of fake European passports, so if anything went wrong they could disown me. It was stupid, but lucrative."

"So why did you come back?" I asked.

"You know how to make sure you always survive . . . ? Make certain that the next risk is bigger than the last. A never-ending game of double or quits . . . "

"Does that really work?"

32

"It did for me, for a long time. I left for Paris because I didn't want to face my responsibilities. Going to Berlin from Paris was a risk when I had no money and didn't know the language. It felt like I was being pursued by a shadow, and the only thing to do, to take my mind off it, was to steal explosives to impress a girl! Whenever the shadow got closer and darker I did something to try and outrun it, or take my mind off it. Like going to the States illegally and running a car-ring. And then, one day in Cuba, I was in this beautiful house in the mountains where I lived with a woman called Elvira, and I'd made a serious mistake. I mean, a really serious mistake, with somebody else's money and status, and this man didn't have a reputation for forgiveness."

Paul laughed and I realised that he was drunk. He continued, " . . . this man made the drug dealer back in the UK look like a teddy-bear. So I decided to run, although I didn't know where to run to. I asked myself, what was bigger and riskier than what I'd been doing? What was the next excessively dangerous thing I could get myself into?"

I didn't immediately realise that Paul wanted me to answer. I shook my head and said I didn't know.

"No, nor did I. I had to think about it. I had a rather convoluted escape route, a change or two of identity, and access to only a small amount of money. I was coming back across the Atlantic when it hit me. I had to finally stop running and confront the shadow."

"The metaphorical shadow?"

"It's always seemed real enough to me. But where to confront it?"

"Pagham!"

"I remembered that Pagham was the dullest, most boring place in the whole world. Miserable beaches, artificial 'Mr. Whippy" ice cream and faded deck-chairs . . . I wanted to see if the shadow would turn up here once I'd stopped running."

"Did it?"

"At first I thought I'd given it the slip. You know how 'nice' it is here in the summer? And quiet, too. It's the dullest existence imaginable. And then November came, cold and wet. And then December, which was worse. It's amazing; so many of these old railway carriages and bungalows are actually lived-in all year round; they're not just holiday homes. There's a whole colony of the sad, disembodied, and disenfranchised living here. I used to despise them, but they're not the problem."

"What is?"

"The shadow, of course. It's out there . . . It hasn't even started doing its work tonight. It's as though it knows you're here and won't reveal its hand . . . "

"I don't understand."

And then, on cue, as though planned by my brother to convince me of his own fears, there was a noise overhead, as if a dozen men in hob-nail boots were running over the roof of the carriage, from one end to the other. The lights flickered and I jumped out of my seat. Paul stayed where he was, laughing.

"What was that?"

"I don't know. I really don't know, but it's been following me all my life."

The carriage, which had been constantly buffeted by the wind, seemed to be lifted off its rotten foundations once more and set back down, but this time it rocked to and fro.

"I don't think we should stay here," I shouted. It was the only way for us to communicate over the sound of the wind and the rain. The wooden walls were reverberating with the noise.

"We have no choice now," Paul shouted back. "We have to sit it out, and pray that this isn't the end . . . Each time there's a storm it gets progressively worse."

"But we can't just stay here and wait . . . "

"Go outside if you want to! If you do, you're a braver man than me!"

"But it's just a storm."

"Is it really?" he laughed.

"Okay, it's a bad storm. We just need to spend the night somewhere more substantial."

"This place has been here for nearly a century. It's withstood countless storms . . . "

There was a sudden blow to the side wall, and I could have sworn that it bowed inwards for a moment. A picture crashed to the floor, and the sound of the water in the aluminium pan was now a staccato succession of ringing drops with barely any pauses. The water was spilling over the side of the pan, spreading over the faded carpet and turning it black.

"They built these things well!" my brother declared, but with bravado rather than real conviction. "As I say, since I've been here the storms have been getting worse. But I suppose this old place will only stand so much, and sometime soon will . . . smash!" He smacked his hands together as he shouted.

"This carriage will soon be so much splintered firewood scattered far and wide over the shingle. They'll find my possessions flung across the salt-marshes, and me facedown in the lagoon. Let's hope it isn't tonight that I finally meet whatever's been following me all these years. But, then again, you'll probably survive; it's not interested in you. You can tell the family how I finally got what was coming to me!"

That was the last thing I clearly remember Paul saying, because everything was drowned out by the intensity of the storm. And then, just as Paul had predicted, the carriage was destroyed. The roof ripped off and there was an instant, vicious change in air pressure. It sucked the air from my lungs, and pulled me from my chair into a roaring, absolute darkness. The violence of it flung me around in what I can only liken to some never-ending train-wreck. Debris flailed me with stinging bites and savage blows, and there were constant punches of ferocious cold air and freezing, salt water. I seemed to hear the sounds of screaming voices and squealing metal. I glimpsed sparks that were immediately doused. The tempest was utterly ferocious and all the time my lungs were bursting as I was smothered and unable to breathe.

I was sure I was being torn limb from limb and I desperately wanted the end to come; any end at all. I tried to put my arms out to protect myself, but everything was out of my control. When I later dared to replay what happened in my mind or, worse still, encountered the horrific tumult in nightmares, I knew the storm had been completely indifferent to me, despite its intense brutality.

I regained consciousness lying half-buried in the shingle, freezing cold and soaking wet. Disorientated, I managed to get up, and I staggered determinedly forward, having no idea where I was going, barely able to stay on my feet. The first light I saw was the unearthly ultra-violet of an insect-killing device in the now-closed fish-and-chip shop. I was amazed to find my bearings after all that had happened, and I made for the hotel.

To my relief the bar was still open, though empty, and the landlord called the emergency services. I was taken to Chichester Hospital and apparently the police, ambulance, and coastguard used the hotel as the headquarters for their search, but there was little they could do that night. At seven the next morning, the search for Paul started in earnest. I was given information during the next day while the search continued, but it was called off that night. They dragged the lagoon the next week, and as Paul predicted, his possessions were found scattered far and wide over the marshes. But they never found him.

I had a broken arm, three broken ribs, and a fractured pelvis, along with multiple cuts and bruises. I looked an absolute fright, but you wouldn't have been able to tell what I'd been through by the time of Paul's memorial service; it was several months later. It was attended by a surprisingly large and disparate group of people from various parts of the globe, and I knew none of them. How they heard about it, I don't know.

Elvira was the only name I recognised. A handsome, older woman with a Spanish accent, she was obviously very distressed by what had happened. She said to me, "I like to think that Paul is still out there somewhere, on another wild adventure."

At the time I disagreed. I said that he had finally found peace. But, later, I decided that I wanted him to have somehow outrun whatever it was that had been pursuing him. After all, there was nothing beyond that shingle beach, he had once insisted. He was my older brother, and something of a hero to me.

Brighthelmstone

I am not sure how old I was when I visited Brighton with my mother; I could only have been about ten or eleven. My father had been dead for about a year and I recall it as the first holiday that we took without him. I remember that I didn't want to go to Brighton. I didn't want to go anywhere. Essentially, I couldn't see the point to anything. I still hated my mother at that time. I think that I blamed her for my father's death, which was completely unfair; his car accident was his own fault. But I was feeling very sorry for myself. My mother's unhappiness angered me: I didn't believe that anybody else had the right to be as upset as I was, and so I took it out on her.

We stayed in a guest house called *Brighthelmstone*, which was on East Street, a narrow, busy thoroughfare just off the seafront, close to the Palace Pier.

"It's a stupid name," I said petulantly as we waited for the landlady to answer the door.

"It's what Brighton used to be called," my mother patiently explained.

We were on the top floor, necessitating a climb of four flights of stairs, and, naturally, I hated that too. For reasons of economy I had to share a room with my mother; a room with two single beds. Whenever we'd been on holiday before, my parents had booked one room for themselves and I'd had another of my own. Now, I resented the lack of privacy, and the unwanted intimacy. My mother appalled me and my refusal to let her even touch me must have added to her agony. I was being profoundly selfish, I can see that now.

After we had been shown to our room, the first thing my mother did was unpack a framed photograph of her and my father, which she set up on the dressing table. It showed them when they were quite young; before I had been born. Then she laid out her never-ending array of chemicals, powders, ointments, and sprays. These had fascinated me; at one time I had delighted in watching her use them. I was drawn to them, I know, because they all seemed improbably exotic. Each one was different, but most had their names printed in gold script on the labels, and all claimed that they had been made in France or other foreign countries. She loved to hear me read out to her the lists of outlandish ingredients they contained. I know now that they were probably all bought at Boots, but they had once seemed so glamorous. By the time we were in Brighton, though, it turned my stomach to see her rubbing the stuff into her skin and painting her face, all in an attempt to make herself look like the younger woman in the picture with my father. And to make it worse, I was always being told how poor we were, and I presumed that these things were expensive. It seemed, therefore, not only a waste of time but knowingly wasteful.

When she started using her creams, powders, and paints in Brighton I had to look away. I took pleasure in going to the window and opening it wide. I knew that my mother hated me to sit on the low sill, hanging out, high above the busy street. It was dangerous, and I suppose I was taunting her, although it pains me now to admit this. I would pretend not to hear her calling me to be careful, or see her walking slowly over to me, not wanting to startle me in case I fell out. I thought that was a good game.

On our first day in Brighton we sat on the beach, which was boring because there were only pebbles; no sand. Under the pier it stank of rotting stuff, but *on* the pier it was more enjoyable. I wouldn't admit this to my mother, though. After a couple of days, because the holiday was going so badly, we took a bus out to some village on the South Downs and walked over interminably dull hills in a light drizzle. I was sure that we were both marking time, waiting for the holiday to end.

And then, one evening, as we walked along Kings Road, we happened to wander into a brash, noisy, brightly-lit amusement arcade near the pier, and for the first time since my father's death I found something that really fascinated me; a large track which allowed up to eight people to race model cars together in slots. It seemed outrageously expensive at ten pence a time, but my mother supplied me with the money for several goes and I was outrageously happy. I'm ashamed to acknowledge that in an instant my apparently profound, overwhelming grief was entirely forgotten.

When my money ran out I immediately considered going to my mother to cajole more from her, but, instead, I waited, watching others using the game, and I found that I was perfectly content to observe. I fantasised that I was driving the slot cars, travelling at incredible speeds, often having spectacular crashes. In fact, I realised that operating the cars was actually less enjoyable than watching others play with them. When I was controlling the car I had to concentrate on speeding up and slowing down, keeping my car on the track, and if it came out of the slot I would have to run around and put it back on again. All this spoiled the fantasies.

On that first evening I spent all my time by the slot racing cars, oblivious to the world around me. Finally I wondered what had happened to my mother, and I reluctantly went to find her. To my surprise she was at the back of the arcade playing bingo. She was sitting in a chair with a strange, mechanical board in front of her, while a bald man in a sparkling suit called out numbers from a raised, glazed booth. There must have been room for fifty to join in the game, but there were only five or six other people playing. I asked my mother what she was doing and she said, without looking at me, "Trying to concentrate."

I watched the game finish, and immediately she put more coins into the slot which reset her board with new, random numbers. As it did so she had time to explain to me, excitedly, that she had won the very first game she had played, and she said she wasn't going to give up on her run of luck. She asked if I was happy amusing myself, and if I had enough "pennies", so I said yes to the first question, and no to the second, which meant that she handed over more coins.

I went back to the slot cars quite contentedly, and watched them until I was hungry. When I returned to my mother she handed me some more money and told me to go next door and buy some fish and chips for myself. This was quite a novelty; I'd not bought food in a café on my own before, but I went and ordered a large bag of chips to take away. I also asked for a cream soda, which I'd always wanted to taste, but had never had the opportunity to try. I soaked my chips in vinegar and salt, which I was not normally allowed to do, and because food wasn't allowed in the amusement arcade, I sat out on the pavement in the garish light of the canopy and enjoyed my dinner.

It was getting dark and the sea beyond the promenade and beach was black and restless. There were a few lights on the horizon, from passing ships, I assumed. By then it had become so much later than we had ever stayed out on previous nights, and I was very surprised to see all the shops still open. They looked so enticing and quite magical in the artificial light, whereas earlier that day they'd looked quite tawdry and down-at-heel.

After I had eaten, I contented myself with watching the slot cars for the rest of the evening. I stood at strategic points around the track, putting people's cars back on when they flew off at corners. I was unaware of the passing time, but then my mother appeared and we went back to the boarding house. It was gone eleven o'clock and I was thrilled to be going home so late. I lay in bed watching my mother with the usual competing emotions of fascination and horror as she got ready, sitting at the dressing table with all her bottles. I also watched the hands of the bedside clock moving closer and closer to twelve, and, finally, my mother finished at the dressing table. She got into the adjoining bed and switched off the light. It was just past midnight, and I felt that some kind of milestone had been passed.

The following morning we went, once again, to the amusement arcade. My mother pressed some more money into my hands and went to the bingo at the back, leaving me standing by the slot cars. I had one go on them, but, as I already knew, the excitement wasn't quite the same as when I was watching other people operate them. The arcade was not yet very busy, though, and as nobody else was playing with the cars I decided to wander off and return later.

It seemed to me to be a very daring thing to do. I had it in mind to visit some of the shops that had looked so enticing the previous evening. After all, I now had money to spend, but suddenly the shops didn't look as wonderful as they had all lit-up in the night. I wandered around an emporium that offered dull rubber rings and plastic windmills on the outside, but inside there was rather more to tempt me. I spent so long trying to decide between a die-cast model aeroplane that caught my eye, and a secret agent kit, that I soon realised it was lunchtime and I was worried that my mother would be looking for me. I hurried out having bought nothing at all and ran back to the arcade. Just inside, walking towards me, was my mother.

"I wondered where you were," she said, but she was not angry with me. She must have only just thought to come looking for me, so I said I'd popped outside for some fresh air.

We went to a slightly tatty restaurant and had a set three-course meal for what my mother said was a bargain price. It was dark and brown inside, and I suspected that this was to hide the fact that the cutlery and crockery were not quite clean. I liked the idea of a three-course meal, though; it struck me as grown-up. It was worryingly quiet inside, though, compared to the cafés I'd visited before. I decided that it was because the elderly diners would probably complain, no matter what background music was played, at whatever volume.

In a whisper I asked my mother whether she was good at bingo and she laughed. She said that nobody was "good" at it; it was down to luck. Yesterday she had been lucky. That morning less so, but in the afternoon she knew she would be winning again . . . She asked if I minded being left on my own and I said no, and that I loved the slot cars, as I honestly did.

When we returned to the arcade, she again gave me some cash to play on the cars. I counted up all the money I had when she was gone, and there were several pounds in silver. It was more than I'd ever handled before, except for my last birthday, when I'd been made to put it all into my post office savings account. I was about to pocket it when a woman asked if I would change her one pound note for ten of my ten pence pieces. There was a queue to get change, she said, and so I warily gave her the coins and she went away. I was staring at the note she had given me in exchange, when a young man came up to me and snatched at it.

I describe him as a young man because, in retrospect, I think he could only have been about fifteen or sixteen. I thought of him as fully-grown then, and frightening at that. He wore a tight-fitting suit, and he had a face that I might have ordinarily liked, but he smelt sour and looked angry.

"Give that to me, and empty out your pockets," he snarled, pushing me towards the wall.

I looked around for help, but suddenly that part of the amusement arcade was empty. I was backed up between two machines offering fluffy toys as prizes for anyone who could operate the crane inside them. I had nowhere to run, and to compound my fear he needlessly produced a knife.

My legs seemed to fail me and I couldn't breathe. I clung to the wall as he jabbed the knife in my direction. Although he didn't quite touch me with it, I was sure I was going to die. I put all of my money into the man's open left hand, dropping some of the coins in my rush to end the ordeal. But this wasn't enough for him.

"Pick them up," he spat, and I did as I was told.

"That's not enough," he said, looking at what I had given him, before stuffing it all into his pocket anyway. "You a holidaymaker?"

I nodded, unable to talk.

"Where you staying?"

"A g-guest house," I finally stuttered.

"Anybody there now, in your rooms?"

"No, my m-mother's playing bingo."

He explained that I was to take him to where I was staying.

"If anyone says anything, we're friends . . . If anyone asks, my name's Tom."

"But I don't have a key," I said, clutching at a valid excuse that made my heart leap with unwarranted hope.

"I don't need keys," he said with a scowl. "We'll walk side by side, like we know each other. And if you try and run I'll knife you."

I didn't doubt him. I hated the idea of taking him back to the guest house, but at least there was very little there for him to steal, and then he would have to leave—my torment would be over.

And so we walked out, just as he said, with his knife concealed under his jacket. I could hardly make my legs move, I was so scared. There were people around us, and I hoped that somebody would look at me and see my fear and growing despair. I wanted somebody to stop us and ask if I was okay. Was I unwell? Where was my mother?

But nobody seemed to notice us. Wildly, I even thought of taking him to a different guest house, perhaps saying I was confused, but I was certain that Tom, if that was his real name, would use his knife if he wanted to. Because he was so much bigger and stronger, I knew that if I tried to slip away, he would catch me in a moment.

Tom complained that it was too far, even though there were only a couple of roads to cross as we walked along the seafront. In East Street I took him to the door.

"*Brighthelmstone?*" he said. "That's a stupid name."

"It's what Brighton used to be called."

I had said the words quietly, remembering my mother's reply to my own similar statement.

The front door of the guest house was on the latch and we entered without anybody challenging us. On the way up he swore at all the stairs, and then fiddled with the lock to our room. He was using his knife, and I assumed he knew how to open the door, like crooks on the television did, but soon he gave up. He looked over the bannisters, to make sure nobody was around, and then shoulder-charged the door. It burst open and he fell inside, onto the floor.

45

That was my chance to run—I knew it—while he was on the ground, struggling. But to my shame I didn't. He got up, came out onto the landing and dragged me roughly inside.

With the door shut behind us I gave up all hope. I was bitterly regretting not having tried to get away. If he was going to kill me, I decided, it should have been while I was escaping; if I was going to die, it ought to be heroically. I was feeling sorrier for myself than I had ever done before.

"Where's the jewellery?" he asked. He threw the knife in the air and caught it by the handle after a couple of rotations. I told him to look for a blue box in the bottom drawer of the dresser. I felt a traitor, but I told myself that he'd have eventually found it anyway. He knelt down and pulled it out, turning his nose up at what he saw inside. He threw the box casually on the bed; his attention had been taken by the picture of my mother and father.

"Money," he said, distracted. "Where's the money?"

"There isn't any."

I was going to add that it was all in my mother's purse, but I didn't think it would do any good to explain.

"Who's that?" he asked, picking up the photo.

"My mum and dad." I don't know what compelled me to tell him, "My dad's dead."

"She's a looker, all right. And available, eh?"

I didn't know what he meant. He now pulled open the top drawer of the dresser and was staring at my mother's underwear. At first I was embarrassed that he had seen it, but to my horror he pulled out a handful of items and then held them to his face and sniffed them. A moment later he had dropped them on the floor and was going over to the wardrobe. There he pulled one of her dresses off the hanger and put his face to where her breasts would be when she wore it.

"Lovely," he said.

"Don't do that!" I told him, and he came out of his reverie.

He grinned at me and ran the blade down the dress. He wasn't cutting it, but that was obviously the threat.

"Please don't do that," I said.

"Or what?" he asked, now letting the blade take the full weight of the dress, and caressing it with his free hand.

I said, "She doesn't look like her photograph anymore. She's all old and wrinkly."

I knew just how horrible it was to say that, and I immediately regretted it. It was so rude, and, really, so wrong. My mother still looked young and beautiful, but I wanted to be cruel to her as well as to him. The effect my words had on Tom, though, was only half-anticipated, and half-understood.

He was angry. He stuffed the dress violently back into the wardrobe, knocking the other clothes off the hangers. Then he swept everything off the top of the dresser; all of my mother's bottles and tubs of exotic creams and powders, her brushes, hairspray, and eye pencils. I backed away towards the window which had been left slightly open. I knew there was no escape that way; I'd stared out of it often enough so that I didn't have to watch my mother at the dresser.

"You're not getting away," said the young man, thinking he'd read my thoughts. In a second he was across the room and, holding me by the neck with one hand, he pressed the blade of his knife into my stomach. The point cut me only slightly, but it felt like a searing flame to my flesh. And then he hauled me up and pushed the top half of my body out of the window. I was balanced right on the edge of the sill, looking up at the eaves of the building and at the sky. I assumed the worst. Gulls were crying above me, and vehicles were roaring far down in the street below. In an absolute agony of fear, I lost control of my bowels. A moment later he swore and let go of me.

For a few seconds I did not know if I was going to fall. The billowing net curtain came to hand and I pulled myself round, grabbed the window frame and got back inside.

"Did you shit yourself?" asked the young man, laughing. "I ought to chuck you out the window to get rid of the smell."

He leant out to get a good look at the street below.

"And it's a long, long way down," he called back to me. He only had one foot on the floor and said something about the air being fresher outside. With all my anger and all my might, I pushed him.

He must have fallen quickly, because by the time I looked out the window he was a mess of arms and legs on the top of a passing lorry. From that distance he looked like a spider after our cat had played with it. And then the lorry was turning left at the end of the street, onto the seafront, and was gone.

I didn't know what to think of what I'd done, but I decided that the most important thing was to make good the damage to the room. I tidied everything up very hurriedly, putting my mother's things back in place. And then I took a clean set of my clothes down to the bathroom, stripped-off, and washed myself thoroughly. When I left the guest house ten minutes later I bundled up my soiled clothes and put them into a rubbish bin on the promenade.

I was shaking when I found my mother, still in the same seat, still playing bingo. There were a lot more people there now, and the blaring pop music sounded louder, and the bald announcer's voice more oily. The endless flashing lights threatened to completely disorientate me, but my mother gave me more money for my dinner and I was able to run back out of the amusement arcade. I promptly threw up on the pavement, and walked unhappily back to the guest house.

I found that I could open the door to our room by pushing on it hard. The lock was still in place, but very loose. Inside it was getting dark, and when I switched on the light I could clearly see that everything was still a mess, despite my earlier attempt at tidying. I don't know how I thought my mother could have come back and not noticed that anything was amiss. Now I took the time, and the utmost care, to put everything properly into what I hoped was its proper place.

I thought that the bottles and brushes, powders, and sprays on the dresser would be the hardest to arrange convincingly. But when I closed my eyes I could remember quite clearly how they had been set out. I managed to make them look orderly and organised.

More difficult were the clothes in the wardrobe. I had put them back on their hangers, but it seemed to take forever to make them look neat. I also had to go through the drawers, folding up the clothes as I hoped my mother would have done. By the time I was satisfied that there was nothing more I could do, it was late, and I rushed back to the amusement arcade.

My mother was standing outside, looking worried. But by then I was quite calm; it seemed to have been a long time since I had pushed Tom out of the window, and my only real concern was that my mother would not realise that anything untoward had happened back in our room.

"I was about to call the police," she said.

"There's no need," I smiled at her, and though my apparent calm was false, so was hers. "Did you win?" I asked her.

"Yes," she beamed at me. "But when I went to find you, so we could celebrate, you weren't there. And that was when I realised how silly I'd been to get so carried away with such a stupid game. What would you like to do next? The choice is yours . . . Anything . . . "

I asked if we could take the train back home, and she was surprised, but after making sure that was really what I wanted, she agreed. We went back to the guest house and packed, and my mother never said a word about anything not being just as it should have been.

Death Makes Strangers of Us All

Katherine Blake accepted that she didn't have any meaningful memories of her past, but often, when she was thinking about something quite different, she could be caught off-guard by a half-remembered face, or a scene, glimpsed at the frayed edge of recollection. She tried to keep a record of these fragments by setting them down in a notebook she found in the small bookshop on the corner of Novotny Street. But to make any sense of any of them was like grasping at smoke. She often re-read the frustrating, brief paragraphs, going over and over them, hoping to re-live the atmosphere of the original impressions. All she knew for certain was that these fleeting images pre-dated her arrival in the city. She was fascinated by the possibilities they offered, captivated by a world about which she was ignorant, but which she knew was utterly unlike her current existence. To begin with, the debris of her memories was always shot-through with shards of vivid colour, whereas the present reality was a black and white world of, at best, ashen hues and tints. The past was busy, full of voices and music, but in the present there were so few people, all sounds were muted, and nothing ever happened.

By far the best way of revisiting her past was in dreams. These were always vibrant but confusing kaleidoscopes. She loved to dream, although she knew that the experiences conjured by her unconscious mind were inherently unreliable. However, even if they were distorted, hopelessly muddling past and present, she treasured them as relating to her previous life. They inspired the longer passages recorded.

The notebook came from one of the very few shops that she had ever found open in the city. Katherine often examined the stock of books in the hope that one, at least, might be written in a language she understood. And then, on one of her visits, she discovered the small volume with its endless empty pages. It may not have been what she was looking for, but she immediately realised its potential. She had no means of paying for the book, or for the pencil she found on the cashier's desk, so she tore out a page and left a note stating her name and address, and she asked to be invoiced. It was the most reckless thing she could remember ever having done, but it quickened her dulled senses to be walking out of the shop with the items. There was, she considered, the slightest possibility that somebody *might* call her back to demand payment . . .

However, Katherine stayed away from the shop for almost two weeks. The potential confrontation that she half hoped for very soon frightened her. But she was unrepentant about taking the book. When she eventually returned to the establishment, cautiously, her pencilled note was still there, untouched. Like everything else in the shop, indeed, the whole city, it was covered in a fine layer of talc-like dust.

By the time Katherine returned to Novotny Street, she had already half-filled the notebook with her scraps and rags of dreams and memories. If read consecutively, the episodes suggested a very surreal and unlikely story, but Katherine was certain that the entries were a key to understanding her present situation. She was certain that she had only to arrange them in the right order for all, eventually, to become clear. And in the meantime, the notebook was a trinket box full of jewels that she could turn over and admire.

Katherine was walking down the deserted street, away from the bookshop, peering in at other windows. She tried all the doors and, as usual, they were locked, but she had not despaired of finding another open, and of it yielding clues. She had come to realise that she must work out her predicament for herself, because none of the few people she had asked had been able to help. Not that there was anyone she had talked to properly apart from Madame Magarshack, and those conversations had filled her with dread. If she was to be honest with herself, Katherine was afraid of receiving an unequivocal, direct answer to her questions. If she demanded of her landlady, "Where are all the other inhabitants of this city?" how would she cope if the woman replied, "They were all wiped-out in a plague", or even, "They left because there was somewhere better to go"? Neither were likely answers, of course, but what was more probable?

Although the city appeared to be deserted, Katherine had seen a dozen different people since her arrival, and she guessed that there were probably several hundred more hidden away, perhaps thousands. They were like ghosts who refused to fulfil their duty to haunt. She had only occasionally been out at night, but had calculated on her cautious nocturnal expeditions that every fiftieth window had some kind of light behind it. Such a rate of occupancy proved that there were more people in the city than she saw on the streets by day, but everyone kept to themselves. However, it didn't account for the million or so souls she *hadn't* encountered.

She walked into the middle of the road. There were cables overhead for trams. There were stop signs, traffic lights, arrows painted on the cobbles, but no moving vehicles of any kind. There were some parked cars, of course, and the occasional stationary bus or commercial vehicle, but it was difficult to see through the opaque windows, and their metallic surfaces no longer offered reflections. They all rested on deflated tyres.

Katherine walked down towards Parliament Square, deciding that it was perhaps best that she come across the truth obliquely, slowly, over time. In the distance, she saw a figure walking in the direction of the cathedral, and Katherine stopped and watched the man. If anyone ever saw her they usually scuttled away; certainly they would never make eye-contact. Madame Magarshack had been the only one who had ever stopped. When the old lady realised Katherine was new to the city, she had invited her to take a room in her tenement. Katherine could not imagine what would have become of her without the old lady's kindness.

The old lady . . . Katherine was aware that most people living in the city were old, although she had once seen a child who had determinedly ignored her as it had kicked a stone down the length of a street. The sound of the stone bouncing off the cobbles had been violent and almost hurt her ears. But, usually, the few inhabitants were elderly and soundless, dusty and grey, like the city itself.

She caught a glimpse of her reflection in a window but moved on, not stopping to study her own image. It had been blurred and indistinct, but not so old, she thought . . . not so old.

She asked herself if it might be best if she just accepted her circumstances? Sometimes she almost succeeded in not questioning anything, and she attempted to make her mind a blank as she made her way out of the commercial district, coming to the residential quarter almost without a single thought in her head.

She let herself silently in at the door of the tenement with the half-moon symbol in crumbling plaster over the front door. She moved through the gloomy hall like a spectre, and put her foot on the first tread of the stair.

"Oh, Katherine . . . "

How had the landlady heard her when she had been so careful and quiet?

Katherine obediently went through to the kitchen where Madame Magarshack was smoothing out a checked tablecloth that should really be blue and white. Madame Magarshack's dark hands were wrinkled like old leather, and Katherine wondered if they were really brown, or perhaps a raw red through hard work. Katherine wanted to hold on to the idea of the colours she had seen in her dreams. She tried to imagine them as existing in the present world.

"You won't believe what that nasty old Mr. Nadim said to me this afternoon," Madame Magarshack exclaimed. "He called me a slattern! He said the stairs were a disgrace, and he could hardly see out of his windows. Well, I told him he could wash them himself."

Katherine wasn't particularly interested in the chatter of her landlady, but she would rather have company than be alone. She sat down and listened, nodding when appropriate, sympathising with the woman. Katherine had exchanged very few words with Mr. Nadim, the tenant in the room below her own, but she didn't much like the look of him when they met at meal times. However, the man did have a point. The stairs could do with a good sweep, and none of the windows in the building had been cleaned in years. Katherine, though, was not going to complain; Madame Magarshack called herself a landlady, but no money ever changed hands, and though she wasn't obliged to do anything for her tenants, she provided their meals. She was a bore, but as Katherine didn't have anything to offer by way of conversation, she could not condemn the woman for rattling-on as she did.

At dinner that evening, Madame Magarshack talked as she served the usual indeterminate bowls of stew to her two tenants.

"I've come down in the world," she complained. "I'm descended from Russian aristocracy."

"Really?" asked Katherine.

"No," said Nadim quietly, under his breath.

"My family lost everything in the revolution."

"That's very sad," said Katherine.

"Tragic," added Nadim, loudly now, but with a smirk which he directed at Katherine. He was always badly-shaven, with wayward clumps of grey bristle left on his chin and under his nose. She wondered if he needed glasses.

"I *am* a tragic figure," the woman said, and sat down to her food. "But I put up with my lot. I never complain."

The other tenant made a "tut" noise, raised his considerable eyebrows for a moment, and continued to eat.

In her room, Katherine turned on the standard lamp, which chased away most, but not all, of the shadows. It only had a very low wattage bulb, but there was little for her to see by it; a wardrobe, a bed, and a rickety, ill-upholstered armchair. As usual the odd ornaments on her mantelpiece, the broken clock, the empty vase and the candlestick, had all migrated to one side in her absence. This still puzzled her, but she no longer found it disturbing. At least they never seemed to fall off when they reached the end.

She sat in the uncomfortable armchair and took her notebook and pencil out from underneath it. A lump of dirty cobweb had become attached to them and Katherine blew it off. For the first time she noticed just how much dirt there was in her room. Sitting low to the ground she could see the clumps of hair in the corners of the wooden parquet floor, and the desiccated remains of many dead flies under the window. There were also some small brown droppings she had not noticed before. Madame Magarshack frequently complained about mice, but Katherine had never seen any rodents, or, come to that, any other animals or birds. An environmental catastrophe was one of the explanations she had considered to account for the world around her.

She read the first entry in her book, describing the scene that repeated itself often throughout her dreams. It was of a large garden by a river where two weatherboarded houses stood at right angles to each other and a magnificent white magnolia bloomed. There were rhododendron bushes with garish green leaves and burning red flowers. In her dreams the garden could be inhabited by various people, but, usually, there was a woman standing at an easel, painting. She was significant, Katherine knew, but she wasn't sure whether the woman was meant to be her mother, some other relative, or just a friend. It was uncomfortable not knowing, but Katherine was certain that she was very fond of her. On waking up she always felt a great longing to return not just to the garden, but to the woman at the easel.

Katherine read through the other entries, finding the descriptions of even the most bizarre dreams more comforting than disturbing, and, as she often did when she read, she started to doze. It was a habit that did not concern her, for, indeed, it seemed to inspire further dreams. These she had trained herself to review immediately upon waking, and to write them down. But this time a loud jolt brought Katherine to consciousness and whatever she had been dreaming was lost. Her ears echoed with a sound that must have been something like a loud whip crack. The whole of the tenement seemed to be settling and dust filled the air. She looked around and could see that the once rectangular room was now slightly out of alignment. It was as though the whole building had experienced a spasm from which it had not fully recovered.

She stood up, worried. To one side of the window the right-angled corner now appeared acute, although narrowed by no more than a degree or two. Conversely, the corner on the other side appeared to have opened up and was now too wide.

Katherine hurried out of her room and down the narrow stairs, nearly tripping, unconsciously knowing that they were now out of alignment and had to be taken with care. She rushed out onto the street, not knowing what to expect, wondering if a bomb had exploded, but everything appeared to be unchanged. There was still dust in the air, but the façades of the buildings appeared to be the same as ever. The only definite evidence of disturbance was a few smashed slates in the road in front of Madame Magarshack's.

As Katherine returned to the tenement the old woman called out, as was her habit. Katherine went in to where Madame Magarshack was washing some bulky material in a big square butler's sink.

"Are you alright?" she asked Katherine.

"Fine, yes," she answered, and the old lady smiled and returned to her work.

"Did you feel an earthquake?" Katherine was compelled to ask.

The old woman shook her head.

"An explosion, then?" asked Katherine.

"When?"

"Just now; a minute ago."

"No. Why?"

"Perhaps I was dreaming."

"I used to do that," said Madame Magarshack.

Up in her room Katherine hid her book and pencil under the armchair once more. After a while she was able to lose herself in thoughts of the improbable garden, imaging how it might be to walk over the grass in her bare feet, and to feel warm in the sun. Perhaps she talked to somebody there? She might have only been asleep and dreaming for a few moments, or maybe it was an hour; she'd often been deceived like that. She usually slept in the chair, rather than on the hard, single bed, and would wake up completely disorientated. Time never seemed to pass regularly; day and night did not alternate as they should, although she had often witnessed the sky turning a matte black in the evening, and brightening to a blank pewter at dawn.

When she awoke it felt like mid-afternoon. Katherine preferred to wash in the mornings, but she felt grimy and decided to go to the communal bathroom. Inside she locked the door carefully and made sure the net curtains over the glazed panels were in place. She stripped before the sink and washed in the tepid water, doing everything she could not to glimpse her dim reflection in the mirror. Not that there was much of the silvering left on the back of the glass to offer any kind of image. But she already knew that she looked thin and unwell; she was not the woman from her dreams, the woman she liked to think that she might once have been.

When Katherine left the tenement the next day she went back to the bookshop with the idea of looking for an atlas or similar reference book that might contain maps. Language would not be a problem, she reasoned, if she could recognise outlines of countries, the shapes of oceans, or mountain ranges. She felt that if she could find a map that showed the city in which she found herself then she might be able to work out where she had come from. As was usual, she did not see anybody else out on the streets. As she walked, she glanced idly in at the windows of the closed shops of tobacconists, milliners, chemists, grocers with empty shelves, as well as the many businesses that she didn't recognise or understand.

She took it for granted that the bookshop would be unlocked, and the moment she entered she started to methodically work her way along the shelves. Most of the volumes were densely printed with text, but it was all Roman, not Cyrillic. She had already worked out that she must be somewhere in Europe, but not too far East.

She was distracted for a while by an illustrated book for children, but she put it back when she realised she had almost forgotten her quest.

Katherine moved methodically from shelf to shelf, but found no maps of any kind. After some time she started to pick up volumes at random to see if the colophon pages mentioned where they had been published, but she couldn't make any useful guesses from the words printed in them.

"London!" she said under her breath. "Paris! Munich!"

They were all names that meant something to her, but she didn't know what.

"Madrid!"

She knew instinctively that she had visited several of the cities, but could remember no specifics. The names flashed by like quicksilver and refused to be grasped. She didn't believe that any of these were the city where she now lived. But if she was "abroad", she couldn't explain how she managed to communicate with Madame Magarshack and Mr. Nadim. If she had been able to muster the energy she would have cried in frustration.

There was a sudden convulsion and everything in the bookshop lurched, books falling from shelves and the dust rising from the floor. It had happened again!

Katherine ran out of the shop and looked around the street, but the immediate area seemed to be as before.

Smoke, though, was rising above rooftops in the distance, down by the Parliament building. Perhaps this was terrorist activity? If so, it seemed pointless. Was it vandalism?

She resolved that she had to discuss the tremors, or explosions, whatever they were, with Madame Magarshack. Not that there was anything the old lady would be able to do about them. Katherine passed the usual shops as she walked purposefully back to the residential district. She had to ask the woman, how come Madam Magarshack had memories of her own past?

"Yes, dear," she said to Katherine. "I remember my mother and father, and growing up as a young girl with all my friends. And then there were the young men who came courting, such handsome young men . . . "

"I don't remember my past," said Katherine.

It had taken a great deal of courage for her to admit this, but the old woman looked at her without expression and said, "Don't you, dear? That's too bad."

"No," said Katherine.

"We all have our crosses to bear."

"I want to know what I've forgotten, and *why* I've forgotten it."

"I'm afraid I can't help. It's probably best not to dwell on it, if it's painful."

"But I don't know if it would be . . . "

"It's probably for the best," the woman nodded sagely.

There was no more to be discussed. Katherine went up to her room and was going inside when she heard a knocking downstairs at the front door. It was the first time she remembered there ever being a visitor. She could hear Madame Magarshack below, bustling out of the kitchen.

Katherine stood on the landing, listening to the voices, not making out words with any clarity until she heard her own name spoken. Then there were two sets of footsteps as Madame Magarshack and the visitor climbed the stairs, stopping to acknowledge Mr. Nadim as he came out of his room on the floor below. Then they continued on up to where Katherine stood outside the door to her own room.

"There's a policeman here to see you," said the landlady, worried.

"Katherine Black," said the skinny man officiously, once he was standing on the landing. He wore a tightly belted raincoat several sizes too big for him, and long, pointed shoes.

"Blake," she corrected him.

"We've been watching you since your arrival. You have spent a great deal of time walking aimlessly around our city."

"Not aimlessly," she defended herself. "I've been trying to get my bearings, getting to know the place."

"You entered a bookshop on Novotny Street," he said, pulling out of his pocket a piece of paper with close-written notes on both sides. It took him a moment to find the place he was looking for. "You stole a book and a pencil."

"I took them, but I left my details so that I could be invoiced for them."

"I did not see anything."

"The note is still there."

"That is most irregular."

"I'm sorry, but I needed the book and there was nobody to pay."

"Needed it? You didn't think to wait until the proprietor was available? What price was on the book? Do you know how much you owe?"

"It wouldn't have been expensive."

"Are you in any position to pay for it?"

"I don't know."

"I would like you to return the book and pencil."

"I can't do that."

"Can't?"

"I no longer have them," she lied.

The man appeared to be both angry and annoyed. He looked at Madame Magarshack for support, but she stared blandly back at him as though she had not been listening.

The man considered his reply for a long time, and Katherine heard Mr. Nadim moving around one floor below, obviously listening to what was going on.

The policeman eventually walked up to Katherine. She refused to move, and so his nose almost touched hers.

"That is not good enough, Katherine Black."

"Blake."

"What?"

"My name is Blake, not Black."

"We take a very dim view of theft in this city."

He paused again, as though waiting for her to say something. He was, though, playing for time, because he was forced to add, "But on this occasion you have escaped charges of theft."

Katherine was relieved, but found herself asking, "Why will the accusation not be followed up?"

She immediately regretted it, wondering why she wanted to prolong the scene.

"*Accusation?*" asked the man. "You have admitted that you took those items. But the matter can be taken no further because the business is no longer in existence . . . "

It was not simply that the bookshop had stopped trading—it had vanished. When she went back, the whole corner of Novotny Street had gone, and it wasn't as though the building had been emptied, or another business had moved in. She was sure that it had been next to the milliner's shop, but that establishment now had a hairdressing salon to one side of it, and on the other was a business selling plumbing fittings. The road that joined Novotny Street at right angles had ceased to exist.

When Katherine returned to the tenement with the half-moon above the door, Madame Magarshack did not want to discuss either the visitor or the disappearing shop. When the landlady was asked, she replied, "I'm sure that I don't know anything."

Katherine sat at the table and put her head in her hands while Madame Magarshack attempted, unsuccessfully, to reassure her.

"Don't think I wouldn't help you if I could, but I can't. I just maintain this building; I keep it clean and cook the meals . . . Don't ask questions, and you will be content enough."

But at dinnertime, Katherine asked Mr. Nadim what he thought. He smiled slyly and said, "I can't really tell you," to which Madame Magarshack responded, "Because he knows nothing!"

But as they ate their stew there was another violent report and a shake of the building. Plaster fell from the ceiling, with bits of lath and other detritus. It fell on their heads, on the table and into their food.

"Explain that!" Katherine shouted, leaping from her chair, and was immediately ashamed by her hysterical outburst. Her landlady was upset and went through to her private sitting-room, shutting the door firmly after her.

Mr. Nadim slipped away like a creaky cat still capable of a little speed.

Katherine went out onto the street and although she knew that something had changed, she could not say what it was. Afterwards, back up in her room, she wondered if the acute angle in one corner hadn't closed up a little further. The wood of the parquet floor was even more uneven than before. It appeared to have lifted and split where the floor-space had diminished, while it was pulling apart where the walls were opening out.

She took her book and pencil from under the chair and went into the street again. From her own building with the half-moon depicted in plaster, she walked back to where the bookshop ought to have been. She noted down each sign on every building *en route*, which included the one with a pig, another with a boat, one with twins holding hands and looking at each other, and another with twins turned away. There was an upside down face, a hand, a boot, and there were symbols of animals, various trades, stars, planets and plants. These all took the place of numbers, and it was quite absorbing to write them all down. When she reached the milliner's and plumber's shops, she retraced her steps and was pleased to see that all the buildings were still there and in the correct order. She had not, though, heard any more explosions or felt further tremors. The next violent crash occurred when she was in her room that night, in bed, asleep and dreaming of the garden with the white magnolia. The beautiful woman had been at her easel, and there was a good-looking young man trying to attract her attention. Then came the apparent explosion that awakened her.

Katherine was out of bed and reaching for the standard lamp, but a moment later she had tripped over it, falling hard on the parquet floor and hurting her wrists and knee. She felt around for the light and switched it on to reveal that *everything* was wrong in her room. It was narrower and taller than it should have been, and the floor and walls now sloped alarmingly in different directions. She could see where her book had slid out from under the armchair and she crawled over to it and clutched it to her chest.

Another loud crack, and more plaster fell from the ceiling, and then there was a ferocious tearing sound as one wall moved inexorably towards her, ripping up the floor at it came, pushing her and all the furniture into the corner until she was crushed and her world went black.

Katherine had her eyes closed tight. Forced into a foetal position, she could not breathe, in part because her legs were crushed into her chest, but also because there seemed to be no air, just a thick, cloying dust. There was also a great roaring commotion all about her, but then she realised that she had mistaken the terrible sound for something quite the opposite; a profound lack of sound, a devastating silence. She only became aware of the difference when, as from a great distance, she heard the calm, restful cooing of a pigeon.

She was suddenly able to gulp in air. She opened her eyes but had to immediately close them against the brightness. She had seen that she was outside, in a garden, sitting on lush green grass. She could feel that there was no longer any pressure, just a slight, warm breeze against her skin. She opened her eyes again slowly, hoping to become accustomed to the light, although it was painful because of the violence of the colours she could see around her. The rhododendron bushes were a tumult of unbearably green leaves and screaming red flowers, but the magnolia was brighter still, fiercely ablaze with intense white blossom that seemed to scorch her eyes.

She was in the garden that she had dreamed about so often. Across the lawn was the woman at her easel, and there was a young man sitting on the edge of a deckchair, staring at the painter. It was all so vivid and bright that Katherine was afraid of not being able to take it in.

With some difficulty she got to her feet, brushing off the dirt that covered her thin, torn dress and her bare arms and legs. She was cut and grazed, but she didn't mind at all. The inconsequential aches and pains confirmed that she was not dreaming.

Fighting a nervousness that threatened to paralyse her, Katherine walked very slowly and unsteadily over to the woman, wondering when the painter might turn and notice her. But as she moved closer Katherine could tell that something was wrong. In the short time she had been staring at her, the woman had not once moved. In Katherine's dreams the woman always had beautiful skin, but now it looked grey and colourless, reminding Katherine of the world that she had so recently left behind. She could see that the woman was like a perfect shop-window model; not real at all.

Katherine turned to the man sitting forwards in the deckchair and he was the same. When she moved closer to him and could see that his skin was almost translucent, like paper. She could hardly bear to reach out and touch his face to find out of what this perfect simulacra of a man was made. When her fingers went through the delicate material of his cheek she snatched them away and momentarily lost control of her whole arm as she shuddered.

She backed away, horrified. There was now a hole in his face, and inside it was simply crumbling, disintegrating, papery stuff. As she watched, the slight breeze seemed to eat away at the edges of the hole that she had made, enlarging it. His face started to collapse—not just the cheek, but the jaw fell away, and then the rest of his head fell into itself like an old, abandoned wasps' nest. Katherine looked at the woman, knowing that if she touched her, then the same thing would happen.

Remembering with horror how the man's cheek had felt, Katherine looked down at her fingers and saw dust on them like ashes. But when she tried to wipe them, she realised that the grey had not transferred from the man's face; her own skin was still the monochrome of the city she had left behind. It was utterly unlike the bright world around her—the aching, gorgeous colours of the garden.

Peering closer, she could see that her skin was actually made of the impossibly delicate material of which the man and the woman had been formed. She was more solid, Katherine told herself, but at that moment she could feel deep inside her chest that the fragile, papery lungs were starting to collapse. She panicked as she tried to draw in deep breaths, knowing that everything inside her was crumbling and falling apart. She glanced down at her grey hands, so recently so solid and real to her, and the light breeze began to lift away the papery layers.

The Man Who Missed the Party

Edward Clarke was staring out of the window of his bookshop, a cigarette held delicately between his long, thin fingers, his unshaven chin slightly upraised. From a distance he didn't appear to be seventy, but up close his skin was not so good; it was too loose and too grey, and his nose and cheeks were patterned with thin filaments of red. He had barely registered the entrance of a customer.

"Can I help you?" he asked. "Any particular author you're interested in?"

"Don't you recognise me?" asked the customer, his voice soft, suggestive of youth.

"Should I?" asked Clarke turning away from the view with reluctance. "Have we met?"

The man had a large, black beard, and a correspondingly wild growth of hair on the top of his head. All that could be seen of his face were the bright blue eyes that peered out from either side of his slightly pointed nose.

"To you it will seem like a long time ago."

Clarke frowned.

"Didn't you once buy a complete set of the works of Rilke?"

The man laughed

"I can see the way your mind is working."

"You have a German, no, an Austrian accent."

"Correct. Now, when did you last meet a man with a beard like mine, who also had my accent?"

"Forty years ago? But that man would now be in his sixties. Are you his son?"

The customer shook his head, obviously amused. He walked around the untidy desk and sat in the proprietor's chair. "You won't have forgotten Terrance Hammond?" he asked.

"Terrance Hammond? I haven't heard that name for a long time."

"You had a brief relationship with him back in 1969."

"Hard to believe . . . "

"With your reputation?"

"And what would that be?"

"People assume you're gay."

"Do they? Even though I haven't had a single relationship since, well, 1969."

"You are considered to be a man of mystery."

"Although I've only ever been staring out of this book-shop window for the last thirty years, buying more books than I could ever sell. My shop is open seven days a week, nine 'til six, and I've never taken a holiday."

"Very odd behaviour."

"I only ever buy my groceries from the supermarket at the top of the road, I always take *The Guardian*, and I never listen to anything other than Radio Three."

"Exactly. People are convinced that there must be more to you than meets the eye!"

"But who are these 'people' who take such an interest in me? Other booksellers? Customers?"

"The rumours are persistent. The received wisdom is that you once worked for the secret services. To buy your silence the authorities gave you enough money to open your shop."

Clarke laughed out loud: "And a private income so that I wouldn't have to earn a proper living? Only in my wildest dreams."

"You are known to speak half a dozen European languages."

"Doesn't everyone?"

The young man smiled: "I know that I do."

"You seem to know a lot about me, but I still don't know *you*."

"Really?"

"Really."

"I've been asking around. I had to make sure I'd found the right Edward Clarke; the man who had once known Terrance Hammond."

"You have found the right Edward Clarke. I spent one night of passion with Terrance and then he was out of my life, he disappeared. He had moved on, I hope, rather than died. I always wondered if one day we'd meet again. And if we did, would I recognise him?"

"Is that why you spend all your time looking out of the window?"

"I promise you that since 1969 I have had other things on my mind than the lovely Terrance Hammond!"

"Of course."

Clarke smiled. He looked out of the window again, remembering.

"I worked in London in the 1960s. I was employed by, well, I won't tell you who, because that might spoil the mystery . . . It was just after Christmas, 1969. A friend of a friend told me about a party. I wasn't exactly invited, but for some odd reason I happened to have a whole case of gin with me, so I was welcomed. I was ten years older than anyone else there, but I found company immediately; Terrance came and sat beside me, and he looked at me with those large, devouring eyes. He didn't leave my side all night. There were famous people there; I recognised Marianne Faithful and Peter Sellers. At first I was a little awestruck; Mary Quant was dancing right in front of where

I was sitting, and there were actors, including the chap with the blond hair who would've played James Bond if he hadn't been such a prude. Susannah York and James Fox were there: the beautiful people!

"Anyway, it was a great party, and I ended up sharing a taxi home with Terrance and a couple of others who were dropped off first. When it was just me and Terrance he suggested that I go back to his flat for a coffee. And so I went with him, and he had this huge room in a big Victorian house. The walls and the ceiling were painted like the sky, with clouds all over them. Anyway, there was just a bed in it, no other furniture at all.

"I never fooled myself that it was the start of a great romance. That would've gone against the prevailing spirit of the time. Everyone was into free love, although I was an old fogey even then. I couldn't have quite been Terrance's father, but I felt like I was at least a generation older than him. When I awoke, I was looking up into the clouds; after a while it was as though I was floating amongst them . . . "

The man in the bookseller's chair laughed: "Died and gone to heaven?"

"Terrance had to leave the next morning to go to Austria, to Vienna of all places, for some modelling assignment that would start in the New Year. Did I say he was preposterously good-looking? Well, he was. And there was going to be another party, a New Year party—a New Decade party! He asked me to come along and I said yes, what the hell? So we went to the airport and somehow he persuaded BOAC to let me have a seat next to him, and it all seemed so glamorous. I mean, a beautiful boy, international travel. I'd never been on a plane before, but Terrance handled everything like it was all very every day . . . I've never flown since, but I remember the serenity of it, being so far up there, removed from the world below. What moved me most was looking down on the clouds. I remember the plane dropping through them, and as we came in to land, looking at the houses and gardens coming up to meet us . . . "

When the young man realised that Clarke had disappeared off into his own private reverie, he asked, "You didn't get a taste for air travel?"

"No. I never went on an aeroplane again."

"What happened in Vienna?"

"When the formalities were over, Terrance hailed a taxi and we were driven miles out of the city to somewhere flat and rather featureless. We ended up on the outskirts of some town or other where the houses were all hidden behind high hedges and fences. There was a party going on, and we were welcome. It was good, but somehow unreal, or surreal, like being in a slightly unconvincing film. It was enjoyable enough, but there was talk of going on somewhere else for yet another party.

"I was tired, though. Once again, I was older than anyone else, and I was happy staying where I was, wherever that was, and drinking whatever I was drinking. The others were all popping pills and snorting powder and had so much more energy than me.

"I was told that this other party was at an amazing place up in the mountains. It had staggering views, apparently, although how anyone was meant to appreciate them in the dark was beyond me. And so I declined to go. The host of this first party was a big man with a huge beard just like yours . . . "

Clarke stopped and stared.

"Do go on," said the young man.

"He looked just like you. He said, 'The house is all yours, man.' And it was; everyone left, including Terrance. I don't think that was quite my plan. I mean, I think I'd hoped Terrance would stay there with me, but he didn't. Perhaps I didn't think to ask him . . .

"And so I looked through their record collection, and over their bookcases, I finished my drink and went to bed. It was late. Well, it was late for *me*, anyway.

"I was woken up the next morning by deafening sirens going off. It was the most unearthly sound. I jumped out of bed and tore outside. The wailing was coming from all directions. I was sure that, as a planet, we were just two or three minutes away from nuclear annihilation. I thought, fuck it! Why didn't I go to that party? Why wasn't I with Terrance? Why couldn't I die while making love to a beautiful boy, or at least happily stoned out of my head like everybody else? I hadn't just missed the party that ended the 1960s . . . I had missed the party at the end of the world!

"I knew from public information films that there would be a zap of light first, and the blast would come later, depending on how close it had been detonated. If it had been far-enough away there would then be a mushroom cloud in the distance.

"I was shivering and naked as I stood there in the garden. I thought about climbing up onto the roof, to embrace fate, to make sure that I stood absolutely no chance of surviving, hoping that for once I really was at the epicentre of things. We all knew that you didn't want to survive a nuclear war.

"But nothing happened. The minutes passed; one, two, three, five, ten, fifteen . . . I was staring up into a blue sky dotted with white clouds which barely moved. There was an aeroplane up there, silvery, almost unmoving."

The bearded man nodded: "The sirens were part of an early warning system. They're still tested once a week. They can freak-out those that don't expect them."

"That's why I could hear relaxed voices coming from the other gardens, and cars occasionally driving down the lane between the properties. The birds just kept on singing. There was a distant cuckoo, and such a strange sense of calm.

"I sat outside in the sun and tried to read a copy of *The Master and Margarita* in a Fontana paperback edition. I have a copy of the very same edition here somewhere. You know the one with the winking black cat on the cover, with the long claws, holding a gun . . . But I couldn't concentrate on it. I kept finding myself staring up into the sky, remembering how it had all looked from up above as we had come into Vienna airport from several thousand feet. I had a kind of out-of-body experience, seeing myself from above, from a gleaming airliner. I was a speck in a chair on a patio, in a garden, in a suburb of some Austrian town I didn't even know the name of. I suppose I was in shock.

"I did start to get worried when nobody came back for hours, but compared to my fear that nuclear war had started, it didn't seem too much of a concern. And then, later that evening, I heard a car. My host came in through the garden gate with his pretty young partner. They both looked shaken, but they were able to tell me what had happened.

"The party had been at the home of a wealthy patron of the arts. Like that party in London, so many beautiful and famous people were there. And great food, wonderful music, and a light-show.

"My hostess explained, through her tears, that there hadn't been any drugs . . . but, sitting behind her, my host nodded his head and mouthed the words, 'Yes, there were.'

"She said it was the prettiest party she had ever been to, with coloured lights all over the house, and in the trees, and there was incense and such a feeling of one 'oneness' and 'spiritual love'. It was like that, she said, for hours on end . . . The most beautiful experience she had ever had . . .

"Word got around that somebody had overdosed. An ambulance was called, and then the police turned up in such numbers that they must have been planning a raid. She said that everyone 'got the fear' and went screaming off into the night, terrified . . . into the trees, into the darkness, and into the snow and the cold of the mountainside . . .

"The police picked up my host and hostess a half an hour later, and took them in and questioned them, but couldn't charge them with anything.

"I asked about Terrance, but they said that they didn't know what had happened to him. He was last seen running down the mountain, into the night, his glass in one hand, a joint in another . . . "

The bearded man behind the bookseller's desk leaned forward and said:

"You stayed for a few days, didn't you? You heard that there had been some really bad acid going around and three people died. Seven or eight disappeared and were never seen again."

"As Terrance didn't come back for me, I borrowed some money from the man with the beard who looked like you. I took a bus into Vienna and stayed with some friends of his. I ended up travelling around Europe, kind of out of curiosity. It took me over two years to find my way back to England, by land and by sea.

"When I got back to London I found a few of Terrance's friends, but nobody had seen him. His landlord had re-let his room a long time before."

"You wouldn't have found him."

"And so, I got back on with my life. I moved to Brighton, opened a bookshop . . . But I couldn't help thinking about that party in the mountains, and what might've happened if I had gone.

"It didn't make the newspapers here, but it did in Austria. There was quite a scandal. I've seen it referred to in books because so many well-known personalities had attended. Everyone else marks the end of the sixties with Altamont in America, but what happened a few months later in Austria was even more significant . . . at least, it was to those who attended the party in the mountains."

The bearded man said, "So, you haven't been staring out of your window ever since hoping to see Terrance's face amongst those of the passers-by?"

Clarke took a few moments before answering.

"No, not really. Terrance was very handsome, and a great deal of fun, but he was always going to move on. If I had gone to that party then perhaps I could have stayed with him a little longer. At least, I might have known what happened to him. What I regret is not Terrance, but the party. Over the years I've imagined just how great it must have been—the wonderful music, the sparkling light, the beautiful people, the mind-expanding drugs, the love . . . I realise that I've probably fantasised about it out of all proportion.

"When I look out of this window I'm not looking into the street. I'm looking up between the buildings, into the sky, through the clouds, to where everything is sunny and bright and calm and serene. I'm looking out of the little window of a shiny BOAC airliner. From up there I don't see myself down here in Brighton on a damp, cold winter's day, but back to where I am just a speck in a chair, on a patio, in a garden, in a suburb of some Austrian town with a name that I didn't ever know."

The young man nodded; "Your memory is good. I was your host in Austria all those years ago."

Clarke smiled sadly and said, "Don't tell me, you've found the elixir of youth?"

"Not quite.

"Can you halt the aging process? Or do you turn back time?"

"Neither. Aging is inevitable if time is passing; as I'm talking to you I'm slowly deteriorating. And time can't be made to run backwards."

"So how does your elixir work?"

"It isn't an elixir."

He took a few moments before he explained: "There is a particular place where time stands still. That's where I usually live."

"A Shangri-La?"

"Of a kind. Think of your life as like a thirty-three rpm record, the needle working its way to the centre where the music will inevitably come to an end. If one of the grooves is damaged it can keep repeating itself, endlessly, never progressing, never coming to an end."

"It sounds a little dull"

"Not if you are in the right company."

The man smiled broadly, or, at least, Clarke assumed that was what had happened; the beard had become animated in such a way as to suggest a smile.

"This might seem a little odd," said the man. "But come inside . . . "

And with that he put his hands to his head, gripped his hair, and yanked firmly to one side. At first, Clarke assumed the young man was removing a wig, but the motion suggested that he was actually unscrewing the top of his head. To Clarke's horror and fascination the man's scalp appeared to revolve twice and then be lifted away. The man put the mass of hair down on the desk in front of him, but from then on he did not say or do anything.

Clark could not look away from the light, empty cavity inside the man's head. After a few moments he moved carefully around the desk and drew closer, reluctantly peering into it. The whole thing was impossible, he told himself. It was an optical illusion; inside the man's head there appeared to be a space that was impossibly large. As he looked down into it, Clarke had the impression of great depth, albeit one filled with something like a swirling mist or cloud.

After perhaps a whole minute, Clarke could still not understand what he was looking at, but he could not look away; indeed, he was drawn ever closer until his face was over the impossible space. When he was close enough, a vacuum suddenly sucked him inside.

The aperture opened to admit Clarke, and then the elderly bookseller was falling and flailing, unable to breathe, unable to see, his ears roaring.

A moment later he was out of the cloud and tumbling towards the earth. The sound in his ears was like a siren, but he had no time to think about that; he was falling like a skydiver now, face down, arms and legs outstretched, the wind tearing at him as he descended at an unbelievable rate. He was falling towards the outskirts of some town; he could see buildings and roads coming up towards him. He could even make out the details of individual gardens, then a specific patio, and at the last moment he recognised the beautiful young man looking up at him with such large and devouring eyes.

It's Over

D avid knew that there would come a time when he would have to meet Salvatore Ruiz. After all, Toledo is a small city and they had several mutual friends and acquaintances. However, David did not expect to meet the man at Matías's flat, and certainly not on a Friday evening for one of their all-night card sessions. It was only six weeks since Amália had left David for Salvatore, and her departure still wounded him to his very soul, not least because she refused to communicate in any way. He did not understand why Amália felt no need to explain why she had left, or to apologise. Refusing all contact only added to the pain and misery he felt.

David had tried to find Amália, of course, to talk to her, but to no avail. She and Salvatore were renting a flat somewhere over the Puente de San Martín, but he did not know quite where. Apparently, even their friends did not have the address.

David dragged his host, Matías, into the kitchen and shut the door behind them. He insisted on an explanation.

"It's time to move on," said Matías. "Make a new start . . . "

"It's far too soon," was David's angry, frustrated reply. "I can't just sit down and play cards with that bastard. Amália and I were together for almost ten years before he came along. She meant everything to me, you know that."

"I'm sorry," said Matías; he was genuinely distressed. "I didn't realise. When she left we commiserated with you, remember? And we all got very, very drunk. And the week after that we did exactly the same thing again . . . But then you seemed to be getting better. And last Friday you seemed to have, well, if not quite moved on, then . . . "

"*Moved on* from Amália?"

"Maybe that's not what I meant to say. You seemed to be *resigned* to what had happened."

"Not at all!"

There was a pause as the two men looked at each other, and then, from the living room, a quietly persuasive voice sang, "*Your baby doesn't love you anymore . . .*"

Drums came in and the song continued, louder:
Golden days before they end . . .

"Matías! I may have *looked* like I was coping, and in control, but it is still very, very painful."

. . . Whisper secrets to the wind . . .

"I still feel like . . . well . . . There's not a day . . . "

. . . Your baby won't be near you any more.

David couldn't concentrate on what he was saying. He wrenched open the door and stormed across the living room. A new verse had started:
Tender nights before they fly . . .

Salvatore stood by Matías's stereo, looking down at the single that was playing, the silver and black label revolving relentlessly.
Send falling stars that seem to cry . . .

David pulled the arm up and it went quiet. He lifted the record off the turntable and turned accusingly to Salvatore.

"That's my record!" Matías pointed out. He was worried that his English friend might smash it over the head of the man with the knowing smirk on his face. "I've only just bought it. The song was in a film at Cinesur just a couple of nights ago."

"It's Roy Orbison," said Salvatore matter-of-factly. " 'The Big O'. We also saw the film—Amália and I. I didn't think much of it; the film or the song."

"I liked it," said Matías. "And the song is haunting."

"Amália liked it too," said Salvatore with a shrug. "It made her weep, but I thought it was just . . . stupid."

At that moment David's anger, his hatred, almost overwhelmed him and he was about to punch Salvatore Ruiz square in the face. Although the man was stocky and strong, and would probably win in a straight fight, David decided that surprise would give him an advantage. But almost immediately his anger turned to something hard and calculating. He had taken it as a taunt that the man had put on the record. But in spite of everything, the small part of the song he had heard *was* beautiful. And when Salvatore said that Amália had been moved by it, David felt that his own situation was not entirely without hope.

"I apologise, Matías," said David, and put the record back on the turntable, this time handling it with more care. He switched it back on and he and Salvatore moved to separate ends of the living room. "It's Over" was allowed to play all the way through, and David appreciated the song as something quite stark and beautiful, although the crescendo seemed to have something of restrained panic about it. He pretended to look over the books on Matías's shelves, while Salvatore contented himself with staring out of the window at the traffic in the Avenue de la Cava.

By the time the song had finished David had calmed down. He would get nowhere by being antagonistic—indeed, he had resolved to be charming, to take his time and assess his rival. It had been a mistake to let Salvatore see how upset he was.

Anthony and Sebastián joined them shortly after the altercation, but they did not seem to sense any atmosphere. They, too, were surprised to see Salvatore among their number, and they seemed astonished at the way that David talked to him in such a friendly manner. Both offered pointed glances, but David gave nothing away. When they sat down at the table David made sure that he was sitting next to Salvatore.

Matías explained the rules to the newcomer:

"We play for very small stakes, and I have a policy that nobody is allowed to lose more than fifty euro in the whole evening, okay? If you want a re-match, a chance to win back your money, you come back next Friday. The main thing is friends getting together, drinking whisky, complaining about their week at work, discussing music, films and books . . . "

"That is fine," Salvatore replied. "Anyway, I play all card games badly."

"Unlucky at cards . . . " said Sebastián, who promptly shut up and would not meet David's eye for the next few minutes.

However, Salvatore was very good at cards, and in no time the newcomer was up by thirty euro, at the expense, equally, of everyone else. It was possible that a further humiliation was on the way for David, but compared to what he had already undergone, this was nothing. And anyway, he consoled himself, his mind was not yet fully on the game they were playing. He was observing Salvatore and had already decided that he was a man of extraordinary vanity. It wasn't just that he was expensively dressed and shod, but his clothes and shoes appeared to be very new. It was nine in the evening and he was sure that the man was newly-shaved, which would explain the strong smell of cologne. His moustache was like a finely sculpted curl of smoke, his sideburns were trimmed to points that were perfect, and his hands were beautifully manicured. However, his hair, David was convinced, was dyed, although his only justification for thinking this was his age; the man had to be in his early fifties but there was not the slightest hint of grey.

David was drinking a fine Kilbeggan whiskey with Matías and Sebastián, while Anthony was finishing a bottle of Glenfarcias. On previous evenings he had been chided for bringing along Scottish whisky, but to everybody else's horror, Salvatore brought out a bottle of DYC.

"Spanish whisky!" the others spluttered, and refused to even try the drink when it was offered to them.

"Too bad," Salvatore said, unconcerned. "That means more for me."

David drank slowly, wondering whether Salvatore would succumb to the alcohol, but that was not the reason why his card-playing finally deteriorated. After an hour Salvatore asked if Matías had any objection to him smoking pot, and his host said no. Salvatore rolled a generous joint and shared it with Anthony and Sebastián. David declined, so as to keep his head clear and his senses alert.

Dusk became darkness, and they played by the shaded table light that allowed the shadows to elbow their way right up to the table. Several hours passed, and fortune ebbed and flowed. Slowly Matías and David clawed back the money that Salvatore had won from them. Anthony lost his entire stake after only an hour and, as was the custom, everyone gave him a couple of euros so that he could come back into the game. Sebastián played as wildly as usual, but somehow managed to retain his stake.

They broke for coffee at about one o'clock and Salvatore appeared to be only slightly drunk, and he was relaxed rather than high. David's whisky was still almost untouched and he felt horribly sober. The smoke caused his eyes to itch and the room seemed airless, even with the windows thrown open. He was still trying to formulate a plan, but all he had really come up with was the idea of getting Salvatore as stoned and as drunk as possible so that he could easily follow him home and find out where Amália was living. He wondered whether he would have the opportunity, down some darkened alley, to give the man a good beating. He didn't think he would have the nerve to tip him into the river if his route home really took him across the Tajo.

When they resumed playing, Sebastián had a run of luck that took Anthony out of the game for a second time, and reduced the rest of them to very little money. But Sebastián was getting louder, and more belligerent, as was his way when drunk. Salvatore insisted on calling his very ill-judged bluff on a single hand and suddenly wiped Sebastián out.

Salvatore celebrated with another generously-made joint, and found that he was now the only one who wanted to smoke it. Anthony left early and Sebastián fell asleep in a chair. David, Matías, and Salvatore continued to play. Quietly and effectively Matías and David took Salvatore's money from him as the man finally succumbed to the effects of the marijuana. It was nearly four in the morning when Salvatore finally lost his stake, but he was inclined to stay and talk. He reminisced about his native city of Madrid, which David knew well from working in Mostoles. It was only an hour away, but Salvatore tried suggesting alternative routes to David that he said would be better than the A42 and M50 that he normally took. But Salvatore was really quite stoned by this time and was making little sense.

David was happy to continue to bide his time. The man had drunk a half bottle of whisky on his own and was on his third joint. His speech was slow and his eyelids looked terribly heavy. Finally David judged it the right time to ask, in as offhand and unconcerned a manner as he could, "How is Amália?"

"She is well enough," said Salvatore.

"I hear you're living on, or near, Calle Cerro de la Cruz?"

"If I told you, you'd try to see her, and she says she doesn't want that."

"I don't know what the problem is. Why doesn't she want to talk to me?"

"It would be too painful for her."

"What about the pain she's causing me by not explaining herself? You know I came home from work that evening and she'd gone. She'd cleared all her stuff out of our house. She didn't even leave a note. And she's never called, never said she's sorry . . . "

"Amália was bored living with you," he said. "She didn't know how to tell you without hurting you. She was trying to save you from heartache."

David very nearly told Salvatore that she had failed. Instead he said, "You can tell Amália that, whether she likes it or not, we do have things to discuss."

"She says she has *nothing* to say to you."

"There's the mortgage, for a start. It's in our joint names and I'm now paying the whole thing on my own. She has a stake in it."

Salvatore waved away David's concern, unable to speak because he had just taken another toke of his joint. After a few seconds he let out the smoke, very languidly, composed himself, and said, "That is not important." He patted his breast pocket. "Here is important—the heart. Love. You care too much for material things like money and houses. She is Portuguese and I am Spanish. We have passion, unlike the English."

"So Amália doesn't want her part in the house?" asked Matías.

David wanted to say that he would trade all of his material possessions to have Amália back, but he was not going to give Salvatore the satisfaction.

At that moment Matías stood up and wished everyone good night. As he always did, he told them to stay as long as they liked and asked them to shut the door behind themselves when they left. He went off to his bedroom, and David would usually have taken this as his cue to leave, but Salvatore seemed content to stay where he was.

"Amália has her moods," said Salvatore, suddenly, as though, during Matías's departure, David had missed a part of the conversation. "You know that."

He was right, of course, but her moods were rarely without cause. David wondered at the implication of the man's words. His first thought was that Salvatore was referring to her unhappiness at moving with him to Toledo in the first place. He had wanted to move out of Madrid but she had not, and for the first year or so she had been unhappy. But then she had made friends, and seemed to enjoy living in Toledo. With sudden hope, David realised that Salvatore was referring to her moodiness with him.

"Amália isn't always very good at discussing her feelings . . . " David said carefully, idly gathering together the cards.

"Her silences can be worse than her words!" said Salvatore, and David's heart leapt again as he recognised the accuracy of the statement. They had argued.

"She can be difficult," David said carefully.

"So beautiful, but so stubborn. One day I expect to come home and find she has left me, just as she left you."

At that moment Sebastián woke up and said, "I haven't seen her since it happened. Is she too embarrassed to see her old friends?"

"No," said Salvatore, as surprised as David was, by the intervention.

"You've got her under lock and key, I expect," said Sebastián, who stood up, preparing to leave.

"I do not need to do such a thing," said Salvatore, annoyed. "I treat my women firmly. They know who is the boss! I need no keys or locks to keep my women."

David would have had to admit, with some shame, that he had mixed feelings at hearing this. He always believed that his relationship with Amália had been an equal one; neither of them would have wanted it any other way. Perhaps it was just bravado that made Salvatore claim to have the upper hand, but if Amália was allowing herself to be ordered around by him, then her humiliation gave David a momentary feeling of pleasure. He did not want her punished for what she had done, but she might realise that life with him had been better than it was now with Salvatore.

David hoped to explore the idea by provoking the man. He said, "Amália likes to have her own way."

"I let her think that," said Salvatore with a smile.

David walked over to the record player and put on "It's Over" at a quiet but calculated volume. As he did so, Sebastián said that he was off home, and Salvatore agreed that he would leave as well.

"Amália never liked me staying out too late," David said to Salvatore. "You'd better be a good boy and toddle off back home."

Salvatore glared at him, as David had hoped he would.

"I come and go as I please," he said slowly, carefully enunciating his words. "No woman tells me what to do."

"Oh, you'll find Amália gets her own way," David said with a knowing smile. "An expensive new dress here, an item of jewellery there . . . "

"No!"

"Oh, come on, Salvatore, be honest . . . You didn't want to see that film, but you watched it because Amália said you should."

"Any woman who gives me trouble . . . " he said, and then slapped his hands together in front of his face.

David was shocked that Salvatore would suggest physical violence towards Amália.

"Don't you ever hurt her!" he heard himself warning the man.

"Or what?" Salvatore laughed. "She is mine now. I tell her who she can see, where she can go, what she can wear."

"Not Amália," David insisted.

"With me she is a little mouse!" he said triumphantly. "You did not know how to treat her."

"I treated her with respect, and love."

"Ah!" he said triumphantly. "There was your mistake."

It was a blow that David should have parried, but for some reason he allowed it to knock him over. He fell into a chair and watched Salvatore leave with Sebastián, quite forgetting his plan to follow the man home. At that moment David imagined Amália lying in bed in a flat he did not know, waiting for *that* man to return to her. Somewhere in Toledo was the woman he still loved, and David sensed that she was unhappy.

"*It breaks your heart in two*," sang Roy Orbison. Then, "*To know she's been untrue. But oh what will you do?*"

David did not know that there was anything he could do.

"*When she says to you, there's someone new*," and the pain was almost overwhelming.

"*We're through, we're through*," sang Roy Orbison, relentlessly. And then, "*It's over, it's over, it's over . . .*" and with every repetition of the words the volume seemed to increase until the room was reverberating with a sound that must have been audible over the whole of the ancient city of Toledo, reverberating both within and without its ancient walls.

It was becoming light outside; the historic Alcázar was silhouetted in sharply defined detail against a sky that was moving perceptibly from coal grey to dark red. Slowly the sun started to pour its crimson glow into the east-facing room where David sat, filling it as with fire.

"*It's over, it's over, it's over . . .* " was repeated as though the record would never come to its end.

As the voice of the singer engulfed David, through tears that he had not realised he was crying, he was aware of Amália standing before him. Upon her face was the most heart-breaking expression of sorrow. It struck him like an axe, cutting through to his very core, and, perhaps, felling his reason.

The first word that came to mind was one that Amália once taught him—*saudade*. It was Portuguese, with no equivalent in English. It was a profound sorrow for something lost, more than just nostalgia, to which was added an emotion more powerful and violent than the French *regret*. The closest word he could think of in English was *hopelessness*.

David was sure he was not hallucinating. He still saw Amália standing before him. He could see her brown eyes and her lustrous, long dark hair. He could see her wide mouth quivering, trying not to cry, but he did not know what she was wearing, or how she had done her hair. Some aspects of this vision of Amália were just too indistinct.

"Where am I?" she asked, as though at a great distance.

"*I* am in Matías's flat," David said, although that answer seemed to be unsatisfactory because he was not certain that he was actually there at all. It was as though they were both together in a darkened room that could be a thousand miles away from Toledo. But even in that room there was a distance between them. Only the endlessly repeated, searing refrain of "*It's over!*" suggested that they were still at Matías's.

He said, "I want to come and help you."

"But I don't know where I am any longer," she replied, looking about her. "It helps to know that you're here, some-where." And then he saw her wrists.

"What have you done?" he asked, horrified.

"I was desperate," she said, from the very depths of her being. "I needed to escape him."

"Why not come back to me?"

"Because *we* were through. There was nothing more between us . . . but oh, why did I ever go to *him*?"

The song had finished and the record player was quietly switching itself off. David's attention was, for a moment, taken by the distended and distressed red sun that had pulled itself up slowly from behind the city walls.

When he looked again, Amália had gone.

David shook his head and stood. Stumbling, he made his way into Matías's bedroom. He woke his friend, demanding to know exactly where Amália and Salvatore were living. Only half awake, still drunk and very fearful, Matías said that he thought, after all, he might know somebody who could tell them. He made a call that took minutes to be answered, and when the voice came on the line he handed it to David.

He didn't know who he was speaking to. He was given an address, and he immediately rang off and called for an ambulance. He explained that a woman's life was in danger.

The post-mortem put Amália's time of death at some time around five o'clock—sunrise. Her body was still warm when it was discovered. Salvatore told the authorities that he had only just returned to their flat. He claimed to have been about to call them.

Amália's death caused Salvatore no end of trouble, not least because David had to explain that it had been the man's behaviour that had alerted him to the danger that Amália was in.

She left no note. Nobody could explain her *felo de se*, and Salvatore went through the appearance of grief for the next few days. Exactly a week later Salvatore apparently committed suicide, throwing himself into the Rio Tajo. It pained David that people assumed that Salvatore had not been able to live without Amália—the depth of his passion had been too much for him. The Spaniard had been playing cards with friends, everyone knew. He had been tired, drunk, and stoned when he had walked home, apparently alone. Nobody saw him fall from the Puente de San Martín.

The Spaniard was described as a hopeless romantic, distraught by Amália's death, and David could not tell them otherwise—he could not possibly explain how Salvatore had fallen. Not that he felt there was much point to keeping himself out of trouble once he had lost Amália.

He remembered her as she had appeared to him that encrimsoned morning. He remembered how the word *saudade* had suggested itself. It was only later when he recalled how she had said, "Because *we* were through", that he realised that the word did not describe *her* despair. *Saudade* was the only way of describing his own profound, aching yearning for a woman he could never have held again.

The Mighty Mr. Godbolt

Tonya matched her pace to that of the sedately departing steam train. She opened the last door of the last carriage with the nonchalance of a seasoned commuter and stepped aboard. Unfortunately the door would not close as easily as it had opened, and, as the train started to gather just a little more momentum, passing beyond the security of the platform, she worried, for a few moments, that the door might not close at all.

She had boarded the train without much thought, and with the guard disappearing through to the next carriage, and nobody else to help her, she became aware of how foolish she had been to jump on the train without finding anyone to sell her a ticket. Tonya took a breath and composed herself. She lowered the window and was able to secure the door with the handle outside. She felt some relief, but it was only now that she wondered quite where the train was going, how long it might take, and whether a return trip would actually be on offer. The gaily painted signs on the platform had proclaimed, "Trains Daily!", "A Vintage Experience!", "Hourly Departures!", and "Half an Hour to the Seaside!", but it had been deserted.

She put her head out of the window and tried not to worry. Michael had told her that he would be exactly two hours, and even if she had to take a taxi back from wherever the train ended up, it was better than waiting in Warrigg. She didn't know why she had ever asked to accompany Michael, especially as she had no intention of visiting whoever it was that Michael was going to see; another *collector*. Unfortunately, the village of Warrigg was comprised only of a few dozen houses and one low chapel. She had hoped to buy a map and go for a walk or, failing that, find a comfortable tea-shop, or even a public house. There were none of these amenities, but it had been a pleasant surprise to find that the village had a working railway station, although, with its unprepossessing single platform, it was probably better described as a "halt".

Tonya noticed a group of children up ahead. They were waving to the locomotive from their back garden, and as she came alongside them in her carriage she waved too. The children, though, had lost interest by this time. She had to withdraw into the carriage anyway when smoke suddenly enveloped her and grit found its way into her eyes. "Smuts," she told herself, pleased to know the correct term.

She took the nearest seat and wondered why, on a Saturday afternoon, the carriage was empty. The schools had all gone back, but it was a bright autumn day and it was odd that nobody seemed to be making the most of the service. The seaside would not be particularly warm or sunny, but there would probably be some attractions, even if it was now the off-season.

Tonya moved next to the window and was able to look down into the rear of more gardens, at washing and rabbit hutches and yet another group of children who, this time, took no notice at all of the train. She assumed that it must be an everyday sight to them; an hourly occurrence, apparently.

It was two o'clock; she made a mental note. She had to be back in Warrigg by four. Michael had insisted that it would take him that long to properly assess the stamp collection that he hoped to buy from some man who lived in the old Station House. Not that there were more than a half a dozen stamps he wanted to keep, he had explained, but he had to be certain of the value of the remainder if he was to sell them on. Tonya tried to not be too annoyed by his collecting, and reminded herself that when they had first married he had also been seriously acquiring ludicrous amounts of matchboxes, cigarette cards and various other printed ephemera. She had persuaded Michael to give up most of this, and the compromise that they had made over the stamps was that he would limit himself to one album. He hadn't been happy to give up the other collections, but to her surprise he had embraced the idea of confining his stamps to the single album. He had decided that with the space for twenty per page, and fifty pages to fill, he would try to collect, exactly, the one thousand most remarkable stamps he could afford. He seemed to relish the idea of "one in—one out", and in various notebooks he ranked the stamps in order of importance and value (which were not the same thing, he insisted). He also made interminable lists of stamps he hoped to acquire . . .

Tonya tried not to think about Michael and his OCD. She knew that her continued annoyance, years after the other collections had been sold, was unfair; he had more than compromised so as to keep her happy. One thousand stamps in a single album was not a lot for an ingrained collector, even if he did devote a great deal of time to them.

Tonya looked out of the dusty window and appreciated the glorious colours of the autumn trees, but, almost as soon as she was able to admire them, the woods disappeared and gave way to flat, featureless fields with only a few derelict farm buildings to relieve the monotony of the landscape. She moved to the opposite window, but the view was depressingly similar. This time, though, her eye was drawn to a large box-like building on the horizon. It was hard to appreciate its dimensions, for there was nothing obvious to give it any scale. Perhaps it was a power station, maybe even a nuclear one. She looked back across at the other window and could see that the land was now rising in the distance, suggesting that she was on the correct side of the carriage to catch her first glimpse of the Irish Sea.

The rhythm of the train relaxed her, but it did seem to be inordinately slow, even though it had been advertised as "A Vintage Experience". She had read somewhere that it now took modern trains longer to travel between major cities than it had done a hundred years ago; just because it was a steam engine, it didn't mean it *had* to be slow. Perhaps the vintage track was the problem? If it was taking too long, she told herself, she could always get off at a station before she ever reached the seaside. Maybe another "halt" . . .

"Excuse me, Madam."

Tonya woke up to see the guard standing before her. He looked concerned.

"Hello," she said brightly, remembering where she was, sure that she had dozed for no more than a few moments. "I wasn't able to buy a ticket at the station. Can I buy one from you? A return ticket, please."

"I'm afraid that this is a private train."

The guard seemed flustered, and incredibly young. He may have had a moustache, but he was hardly sixteen, and he looked quite uncomfortable in his ill-fitting "period" uniform.

" 'Trains Daily!'," she quoted. " 'Hourly Departures!' 'Half an Hour to the Seaside!' "

"Normally, yes, but not today. That's why nobody was at the station to sell you a ticket."

"Then you should have put up a sign saying 'No Trains Today!' "

"We did."

"I didn't see it."

"Obviously not."

"Who is in charge?" she asked officiously, but then realised that the young man's "Obviously not" hadn't been meant as a rebuke.

"I don't know," he said, looking over his shoulder towards the next carriage. "I'll ask. I'll see if I can find Mr. Roberts. He'll know what to do."

"I don't want to cause any trouble. Can't I just pay for a ticket and sit here quietly?"

"I don't know. You see, as I said, this is a private train today."

The guard left with alacrity, and Tonya turned back to the window. The strange box-like building was now almost out of sight, but the fields were as dreary as before. It was reclaimed land, judging by the drainage ditches. The sudden appearance close to the track of a broken-down caravan seemed to underline the impermanence of the landscape. The next field included a few thin cows, some of which appeared, at first, to be watching, but she noticed that their heads did not follow the movement of the train.

The door opened at the far end of the carriage and the young guard reappeared, now followed by a middle-aged man with his hair brilliantined in just the same way as Tonya's grandfather in his black and white wedding photo.

"How did you get in here?" he asked. The can of beer in his hand worried Tonya.

"I appear to have made a mistake," she said, smiling at him hopefully.

The man sat down opposite her, heavily.

"I should say so. This isn't a train you should be on."

"Why not?"

"It's Mr. Godbolt's train," said the young man.

"Oh yes," agreed the other, taking a swig from his can. "This is certainly Mr. Godbolt's train. Mr. Godbolt's *last* train."

"Perhaps I should apologise to him?"

"You could try," said the man. "But he isn't in any position to hear you."

"Why not?"

"Because he's passed away," said the guard.

"He is taking his final journey," said the man with the can. "He has clipped his last ticket, set his ultimate signal, pulled the whistle for the very last time . . . "

"I'm sorry to hear that. Who's in charge, then?"

"A good question!" said the man, now staring at his can, as though it had something important written on the side of it. "The shareholders will have their say, I expect. In the past everybody simply did what Mr. Godbolt said. He was the man of vision. He was the one who got things done. He fired us up . . . "

The young man looked away, embarrassed, as the older man wiped a tear from his eye, before taking a restorative swig and continuing:

"Mr. Godbolt used to travel this line as a lad to get to school, but Mr. Beeching axed it in the nineteen sixties. Godbolt resolved that he would bring it back into use, and for a couple of decades he tried writing to parliament, and raising the money to buy the line, all to no avail. But then, in the nineteen nineties, he founded our Railway Preservation Trust. He worked seven days a week, for just over ten years, and, despite opposition from all sides, he finally got permission to re-open the line. We ran our very first train just over two years ago."

"He was an inspiration," said the guard.

"As the lad says," the man agreed, "Godbolt was inspirational. We all looked up to him. He was a, well, a colossus . . . a titan."

"I'm very sorry for your loss," said Tonya.

"Everyone's loss."

"Would you like to see him?" asked the lad. "It would be all right, wouldn't it, Mr. Roberts?"

"Why not!" said the other. He stood up, extending a hand.

"See him?"

"Yes. He's laid out in the buffet car."

The mental image created in Tonya's mind was an unfortunate one, and it meant that she initially declined, explaining how she didn't want to intrude on private grief. She imagined the mighty Mr. Godbolt on the counter of the buffet car surrounded by tuna and egg sandwiches, perhaps cut into triangles. There would be sprigs of parsley.

The young man urged her to consider following them. The older man insisted it would be quite all right. Tonya was mainly worried because she had never seen a dead body before, despite having attended several funerals. Was it normal practice in this part of the country? The two men really did seem to want her to see the late Mr. Godbolt.

What Tonya hadn't expected was so many other men in the buffet car, all similarly dressed in archaic railway uniforms, all talking loudly while drinking, like Mr. Roberts, from cans of beer. There were sandwiches on the counter, triangular ones, but Mr. Godbolt was not laid there. He was in an open coffin on one of the tables, the head end intruding slightly into the aisle.

In life Mr. Godbolt may well have been a colossus, a titan even, but in death he was a small man with badly dyed black hair and a moustache that had obviously inspired the young guard to grow his in the same style.

"He looks very peaceful," Tonya said, wondering what other remarks might be appropriate.

"He fought a long, hard battle," said a tall, thin man with bushy eyebrows. He was staring down into the coffin quite intently. He also appeared to be drinking a large measure of whisky from a cut-glass tumbler. "But he won!" said the man. "Mr. Godbolt can sleep comfortably, knowing that his line is safe, and valued."

"That is some comfort," Tonya replied.

"You knew him?"

"No, not at all. I'm on the train by mistake."

"Then it is a delightful mistake," said the man, rather oilily. "My name is Brian."

"I'm pleased to meet you, Brian."

"Dennis Brian," he continued. "Would you like a drink?"

"I would, thank you."

"But you don't want the rubbish they're swigging," he said. He revealed a half-bottle of Bells in his inside jacket pocket.

"I'd love one," she said.

"But there are no glasses. The silly fools who run the buffet forgot. Here, take some from this."

Tonya really didn't want to share his glass, but felt it would be rude to decline. Under his gaze she took the tumbler and went to take a sip from the side that he hadn't been drinking from. Whether it was the motion of the train going over a point, or someone in the crowded buffet car bumping into her, the alcohol sloshed out over her chin.

"You'll not be used to whisky," said Dennis Brian. "It's a man's drink, really."

The comment annoyed Tonya; she knew and liked whisky. But it was the mention of men that suddenly bothered her. Of course she had been aware that she was the only woman in the buffet car, and the cheery crowd was not at all threatening, but her self-confidence suddenly deserted her and she could only consider how she might return unobtrusively to the other carriage.

"Godbolt lived in Warrigg all of his life," another man told her. He had on a bright neckerchief and looked like the train driver.

"Really," she replied, politely.

"He said he'd never move away all the time he was fighting to re-open the line."

"He said that!" replied Dennis Brian. "But then, why would he move away once there was a working line again? After all his work!"

The two men laughed.

"He lived in the station house," said Mr. Roberts, who moved awkwardly between the seats and the coffin. "His bedroom overlooked the platform. Those last few weeks, while he was ill, he sat at the window, still making sure everything was run the way it should be."

"The station house?" asked Tonya. "My husband is meant to be seeing him today, to buy a stamp collection."

"He collected 'railway stamps'," said Roberts. "He showed me once."

"What are 'railway stamps'?" asked the man with the neckerchief.

"Stamps issued to pay for a letter or a parcel sent by rail. Godbolt's collection had examples from private and state railways, from home and abroad. Did you know the first railway stamp was issued in England in 1846?"

"Like those stamps he had made up himself? He sent away for them."

"Exactly the same."

"He had his own head on them . . . "

"My husband must have been corresponding with Mr. Godbolt," Tonya continued. "He's . . . "

"He's too late!" said Brian. "As you can see, Mr. Godbolt is here with us!"

"He'll be looking for me in Warrigg."

"What, Mr. Godbolt?" asked Brian.

"No, her husband," said Roberts.

"*He* won't have found him," said the other man. "But *you* have!"

The man and Brian found this very funny, and the cut glass tumbler and can of beer were knocked together by way of a toast.

"I need to get back to Warrigg."

"Then you're going the wrong way," said the other man. "This is Mr. Godbolt's train. We are going to the terminus and then, well, that's it. Where is there for any of us to go after the terminus?"

"You will be going back to Warrigg, won't you?"

The man in the neckerchief looked down into the coffin and asked, "What is beyond the terminus, Mr. Godbolt?"

The young guard suddenly piped up from behind Roberts, "The undiscovered country from whose bourn no traveller returns."

"A one way ticket," said Roberts.

"Precisely," said Brian. "There is no turning back."

"One could jump off the train," said Tonya.

"One could," said Roberts. "We are not going at any great speed."

"I noticed that," said Tonya. "Why are we going so slow?"

"Nobody wants to get to the terminus too soon," said the man with the neckerchief.

"Nobody!" said the guard.

"Not when there is still beer, and plenty of sandwiches."

"Aren't you meant to be up front?" asked the guard.

"What and miss the party?" asked the driver.

Tonya pushed her way back through the crowd of men and passed into the last carriage. She had expected to be followed, but nobody came after her. She put her head out of the final door and realised that they really were not travelling very fast at all; no more than a brisk walking speed.

With the same lack of thought with which she had boarded the train, she now opened the door and jumped out. It was a greater distance to the ground than she had bargained for, and the forward momentum meant that she fell sideways and rolled through long grass and nettles down a slight embankment. She was, though, unhurt, and climbed back up to the track, to see the train slowly moving away, the last door of the last carriage half open, waving to her.

All around were the same featureless, sad fields, and the only landmark in the distance was the strange box-like structure. She looked at her watch and saw that it was half-past two. She calculated that if she only walked back at a third of the speed at which the train had been moving, she should still be back at Warrigg by four. It was difficult to walk along the track-bed of sleepers and gravel, but she soon established a rhythm.

It was a long and uncomfortable walk. She really could find no stride pattern that fit with the sleepers, and all the way back she berated herself for the recklessness with which she had boarded the train in the first place. The whole time she rehearsed in her mind the various explanations and excuses she would have to offer Michael. She worried that he might have called the police when he realised that she was gone.

When the Station House finally came into view, and Warrigg station itself, she squinted but could not see anybody looking for her. The platform was empty, apart from its bright painted boards. The first she was able to read clearly said, "No Trains Today".

"Hey, Tonya!"

She turned and there was Michael at the car, slamming shut the boot.

"I'm sorry," she said as she walked up to him. "You must have been waiting for me for ages."

"No," he said. "I've only just escaped. The old boy was impossible to get away from. Come on, get in. If he sees you he'll be inviting us both back in, offering us tea."

Tonya was as pleased to leave Warrigg as Michael seemed to be, although he was excited and happy.

"He's an amazing man," Michael explained. "Larger than life. I wanted some good examples of 'railway stamps' for my album, and that was his speciality. You know, they were issued for post that was sent by rail. He had some printed up for use on the railway that runs past his house. I'm not sure if I'll keep any of those, though."

Tonya was pleased that Michael didn't keep Godbolt's own "railway stamps". He described the man as larger than life, but the face on the stamps was of the small man with the moustache she had seen in the coffin in the buffet car of a train slowly heading for, but not having quite reached, the terminus of the line.

One Man's Wisdom

Henry was back in his childhood bedroom for the first time in ten years and it was as though he had never been away. The wallpaper was the same and the bedspread was the one he remembered from his youth. All of his old books were still in the case under his window, but when he stood up from them and pushed aside the yellowed net curtains that smelt of dust and decayed sunshine, the view had changed. He looked out across a wasteland of rubble where once the engineering works had stood. As a boy he had always heard the machinery rattling away over there, night and day, under the black-tarred asbestos roofs, steam rising from randomly-placed little tin chimneys, oily water ejected from pipes into the sluggish stream that ran alongside it. For the first time he wondered just what it was that they had manufactured in there? He had never known. He had never thought to ask during all those years he had been growing in the flat above his father's ironmongery shop. He resolved that he would find out while he was visiting.

Looking down into the ironmongers' yard Henry saw Kingsley going in at the rear entrance to the shop; he had only glimpsed the old man's back, but it could not have been anyone else. Kingsley was the only employee left.

Henry looked sideways across the yard to the dilapidated green-painted store, an ugly, ramshackle building of timber and tin that hadn't been used in years. Like the engineering works this too was to be demolished, but it seemed such a shame that the shop and their home would also have to be levelled. Although he hadn't been back for so long, there had always been some security in knowing that it was all still there, his childhood preserved in those few, admittedly ugly, buildings. Nobody seemed to know who was acquiring all the land and tearing everything down, not even his father who had agreed to the sale.

"What do you care?" Kingsley had asked Henry earlier that afternoon when he had ventured into the shop. "You've never been a part of this place. Nor's your father, not really. It's always been called a 'family business', but he's made sure that it ends with him."

Henry didn't feel confident that age, or the counter between them, was any barrier to Kingsley coming over, taking him by the scruff of the neck and throwing him out. He had done it before, when Henry had been younger.

"I think I'd better go," he said, putting his hands up in submission and backing out of the shop. He wondered why he had ventured inside in the first place.

"You're as bad as your father!" Kingsley had called out after Henry. "You think you're too good for the rest of us."

Much of what the man had said was correct, of course. Henry's father had never concerned himself with the shop-floor of the ironmongers, even when it had been a thriving business and employed a half-dozen sales assistants. He had always hidden himself away in the office at the back with the paperwork; invoices and receipts piled high on all the surfaces, kept on spikes and ludicrously threaded on string. He had refused to let anyone in the office in just the same way that Kingsley now didn't want anyone else in the shop with him. They were both as bad as each other.

Dinner that evening was a cheerless affair.

"These days it's difficult for an old-fashioned ironmongers to survive," Henry's father pointed out. They were in the cold dining room that had been opened up and dusted especially for Henry's arrival. The plain pork chop, peas, and potatoes with a little puréed apple were what his mother always mistakenly assumed was his favourite meal.

"Ordinary customers never come to this end of town, and the trade business has slowly dried up. They're reducing the whole area to rubble before it's completely redeveloped."

"And nobody knows who by?"

"No, but it's meant to be progress . . . "

"How much are they paying?"

"That's for me to know," said his father.

There was what might have been an uncomfortable silence. Henry didn't care much.

"The business itself has no value," said his father. "But the land's worth more than you'd think. The engineering works had ten times the land we've got, but *we* have the access off the main road. They'll tear down the shop and the old store, and they'll get their deliveries through here rather than going through the town itself. Where we are will just be a place for trucks to turn around and unload."

"So it's manufacturing of some sort?" Henry asked.

"Your father doesn't know," said his mother. "He's guessing. It'll be a great shame, but we must move with the times. Three generations have run the ironmongers. I was always surprised that you didn't want to come into the business?"

"It never appealed," Henry admitted, looking down at his food. "And working alongside Kingsley . . . "

"I suppose that would have been enough to put anybody off," she said. "You do realise you're not the only one to be frightened of him?"

"I am not frightened of Kingsley!" his father spluttered. "It's just that he's been working here long enough that he deserves our respect."

"Pah!" she replied, with a surprising depth of expression.

Henry was quite sure that his father had never wanted his son to work alongside him; perhaps he feared that Henry would have argued with him just as he had done with his own father.

"If Henry had joined the business," his father considered, although some minutes had passed, "Kingsley wouldn't have been a real concern. I'd have let him go like the rest of the staff."

Henry's mother recalled: "There was talk, at one time, when things seemed to be picking up again, of getting Kingsley an assistant. Just think, that could have been Henry . . . "

Kingsley had always been a part of their lives, and never a very friendly part. When Henry had been growing up above the shop he would see the man arriving for work every morning, going through the routine of unlocking the chain across the entrance to the yard before opening up the shop itself. Once inside his first job in the winter was to fight to get the old paraffin stove lit. If he saw Henry he would scowl, and even when Henry was older, and nearly as tall as him, he was still frightened of the older man.

Henry couldn't believe that anybody could call Kingsley a pleasant fellow. He was something of a joke among the local tradesmen who went to him for their supplies, but they did respect his knowledge. Henry couldn't remember questioning the man's presence any more than he had the engineering works; when he was young he simply accepted Kingsley and everything else around him. He never considered that one day it would all be gone.

"What did they make in the engineering works?" he asked.

"I don't rightly know," his father replied, shrugged and went back to his food.

"It was strange the day they closed down, though," his mother mused. "It just suddenly went quiet, and I thought something had gone horribly wrong. It's strange what you get used to."

"I suppose you could ask Kingsley," suggested his father.

"I could . . . "

"But he's not in the best of moods. As you can imagine, he isn't pleased we're selling up."

"I tried talking to him earlier."

"He's been with the firm since he was fourteen," Henry's mother pointed out.

"As he has never ceased to remind me . . . " said his father.

"He won't go without a fight?" Henry asked.

"No, though he's well past retirement age. I'm happy to pay him more than I'm legally obliged to, but at the moment he's just refusing to accept it."

"He's holding out for more?"

"He claims it's not the money."

"So what are you going to do?"

"It's not really my problem. When the contracts are signed he can chain himself to the green store if he wants to."

"Why the green store?"

"He insists that I can sell the shop and trade counter, but I mustn't sell the green store."

"Why not?"

"Perhaps you should show your son what's in there," Henry's mother suggested, "before it's torn down?"

"Later."

"Why not now?" Henry asked.

His father looked at his watch: "Give Kingsley time to lock up and leave for the evening."

When Henry had finished eating he went to the window and looked out, down the main road. A few minutes later he saw the old employee putting the chain across the entrance.

Even from above Henry could see why his school friends had always called the man "Lurch". He was tall and had a large face with a lantern jaw. Clean-shaven, he never showed a sign of stubble, and his thinning hair showed off the cold white skin of his scalp. He always wore an old-fashioned long, grey coat to protect his clothes from the dirt and grease of the shop, and this seemed to add to his strangeness. On his breast pocket there was an embroidered logo that the business had stopped using thirty years before. Henry had always known him to smell of Swarfega and paraffin, and he never ate lunch. With hindsight he could see that these were really only minor eccentricities, but as a child he had always thought of him as a deeply worrying character.

He watched the man check that the padlock was secure before walking off up the road towards the brighter, more modern and successful shops.

"He's gone," said Henry, and his father nodded. He had finished eating and exchanged glances with his wife, who nodded to suggest that he should go. He dutifully got up from the table and Henry followed him to the hall. They put on coats and shoes before going out and down the steps that led into the passageway. In the yard his father pointlessly tried the handle on the back door of the shop.

"I should have torn the store down years ago," his father said as they approached the green building, which was dark and forbidding against a cold evening sun. "We could've sold this part of the site a long time ago, but my father wouldn't let me."

"Why didn't you just sell it after he'd gone?"

"When you see inside you'll see why."

"I was never allowed inside," Henry pointed out. "I was told it was too dangerous, and derelict."

"Well, it still is dangerous and derelict. Your great-grand-father built it when he gave up with the forge and stables.

He ran the contract for laying the local gas main, and this was where they kept their materials and equipment. It's still half full of it."

Henry's father looked around to make sure he was not observed, and produced a key which he slipped into the lock and turned. He hurried Henry inside and in the dark he locked the door behind them.

The little light from the high, grimy and cobwebbed windows showed them to be in a two storey-height space with corridors of industrial metal racking. There were impressive cobwebs high up in the corners of the roof, but somehow the place failed to echo as Henry felt it should. It smelled of metal and oil from the previous century

"Don't touch anything," his father insisted as they walked past huge cast-iron joints for heavy-duty pipe-work. "It's not going to fall on you, but it's filthy in here."

At the end of the corridor of shelving was another door that led into a single storey room. The windows to the street were boarded up, but a single bare bulb gave a dim illumination. All around was the equipment that had presumably been used for the laying of the pipes. Much was hidden under black tarpaulin, but where it had fallen away Henry could see the barbaric, rusting forms of the machinery. The next door was locked, but again Henry's father had a key. It was bolted as well, but on their side of the door. It grated, but when he was able to pull the door open his father drew in a breath and let his son go inside before him.

It was darker still, and it took a few moments for his eyes to adjust. This end of the building had no windows, but there were translucent sections in the metal sheeting of the roof. They gave the space a curiously green, underwater atmosphere, and illuminated the strange sight of writhing pipe-work that confronted him.

"What the hell is that?" Henry asked. It looked, to his mind, like some monstrously complicated sea-creature created by a Victorian engineer. It was a vast mass of cast-iron tubes that ascended organically from the floor through the full two storeys to the roof. The pipes wrapped around each other and were forever going into or out of the main body of the bizarre creation. The joints, plates, brackets, and junctions were all fixed with a myriad of bolts and rivets.

After he had taken his time to appreciate the strange sight, Henry again asked his father what it was.

"Heaven only knows," he said, staring at it himself. "Or rather, there is one person who knows."

"Kingsley?"

"Exactly."

"Does it do anything?"

"I don't know that it does. It'll sound stupid, but there appears to be a control panel around the other side. It looks like something out of a Jules Verne novel, but I can't see what on earth it could do, even if there was power to it."

Henry walked closer to the metal rail in front of the great accumulation of pipes and looked down, realising that it did not sit on the floor, but seemed to travel on downwards into darkness.

"How far below us does that go?"

"I reckon about a hundred feet."

"What?"

"If you shine a torch down you'll find that the whole thing tapers away from the sides, towards the base."

"And it's always been here?"

"Before even my father's time."

"What did he make of it?"

"I don't know; he would never say."

"Over the years you must've wondered what it was?"

"Of course. The only plausible explanation is that it's a kind of folly, or sculpture. The whole thing is made entirely of old gas pipes. It's constructed out of the materials left when they'd finished laying the main."

"But Kingsley won't explain it?"

"No. He refuses to. And he claims that he didn't build it—just that he maintains it."

"How can he maintain something that doesn't do anything?"

Henry's father shrugged.

"What does my mother think of it?"

"When she first saw it she was so worried by it that she's refused to ever come back inside."

Henry shook his head and started to slowly walk around the giant construction, wondering what on earth to actually call it. He wanted to describe it as a "device", but that would imply that it did something, as would "mechanism" or "contraption". It was certainly much more than just an "object".

"But removing this . . . whatever it is . . . " he started to ask.

"It'll be a mammoth task, yes. The developers have negotiated a certain amount off the asking-price if they have to do it themselves. It has some scrap value, of course, but the work involved in dismantling it . . . "

"I'm sure it can be taken down, but do the developers know about the pit it stands in?"

"Yes, I smuggled one of their people past Kingsley last month and he took a long look at it. He said that because it'll only be traffic going over it into their car park they'll effectively build a bridge over the void."

The thought struck Henry:

"Somebody must have excavated it in the first place . . . "

"Someone? It would've been the work of a dozen men, at least, over a long period of time. But no local historian has ever mentioned the digging of so vast a hole. I've a feeling that it might have been done *after* the building was put up. The sides of the pit seem to be shuttered concrete; they must have gone down in sections, shoring up the sides as they went."

A half way around the thing Henry found what his father called the control panel, and that is exactly what it looked like, with dials and levers attached. It was essentially a large wooden board and from the back of it a galvanised metal tube disappeared into the mass of pipe-work; presumably this would carry any wires, or cables, if it had any.

"Can I flick the switches," Henry asked, "and turn the dials?"

"By all means. Nothing happens, I've tried. Afterwards, though, put them back in the position you found them."

"In case Kingsley comes in and finds we've been playing with his machine?"

"Exactly."

That night Henry lay in his old, narrow bed, thinking of the giant machine only a hundred feet away in the old green store. What worried him was not knowing what it was capable of. He had suggested to his father, jokingly, that he try and sell it as a piece of modern art, but his father did not find it funny. He told his son that he was convinced, intellectually, that it was simply scrap metal, but the attitude, not only of Kingsley, but his own father, made him wary of it. He was relieved to have sold the building so that now, when it was dismantled and removed, it would be somebody else's responsibility.

Henry dreamed about the device that night, but he did not realise that he had done so until some minutes after he had awoken. His dream had been of running up and down circular corridors, and moving between them, trying to go in a certain direction and failing because they kept changing direction. He had a good sense of direction normally, but he was completely disorientated in his dream. It took some thought before he realised that he was meant to have been *inside* the great device in the green store.

It was his intention to leave as soon as he could the following morning. There was no rush to go back to the city where he worked, but his life was there, not in the old town where his parents still lived. He hurried his breakfast as they all sat in silence, his mother making small-talk. They all heard the chain in the yard and his father said something about Kingsley in an undertone.

"Why," asked Henry, "have you spent all your lives tip-toeing around one peculiar old employee. Why are you frightened by an accumulation of old pipes that some men put together in a shed when they found time hanging heavy on their hands?"

They had no answer.

"I would like the key to the green store."

"Why?"

"I want to go and take another look at that . . . thing," Henry explained.

"Kingsley's bound to see you going in."

"I know," said Henry, with assurance than he felt. "Perhaps it would be more considerate if I told him of my intentions first?"

His father looked puzzled, then worried, but after some thought he passed his son the keys. Henry was surprised that he gave them to him so easily, but then realised his father actually wanted a confrontation with Kingsley. Not that he had the courage to do it himself.

"You're welcome to join me," Henry suggested as he stood up.

"I'll be along in a moment," was the reluctant reply.

When he was outside Henry went around to the front of the shop and looked in. He could see Kingsley through the window, already at work behind the counter. He had a customer with him, and Henry thought that perhaps he should wait for the man to finish, but instead he opened the door and held up the key.

"I'm going to take a look in the green store," he said simply, and shut the door again before Kingsley could reply.

Henry walked quickly across the yard and let himself into the building. It was as he was shutting the door after him that he heard Kingsley call. Henry hurried down the length of the first room, past the racking, wanting to make certain that he was through to Kingsley's bizarre contraption before the old man could catch up with him. Henry wanted to be calm, but his heart was thumping and when it came to opening the second door he fumbled with the key and lost some of his advantage. Kingsley was in the building by that time, running through the first room, calling out to him.

Henry made it into the last room, the enormous space of subaqueous gloom, before Kingsley could do anything to stop him. The enormous bulk of the pipes loomed up before him and took shape as his eyes adjusted.

"What are you doing in here?" Kingsley demanded, or perhaps pleaded.

"I'm going back this morning," Henry explained, as steadily as he could. "And I wanted to take one last look at this."

"You've seen it before?"

"My father showed it to me last night."

"He shouldn't have done that."

"No? Why not?"

"He just shouldn't have."

"Well, it's all going to be taken down," Henry said, enjoying his heartlessness, recognising that he was taking pleasure from having the upper hand with the old man for the first time in his life. All the petty, stupid indignities, the terrors that he had inflicted on Henry as he had been growing up, could be repaid in that single moment.

Henry walked over, leant across, and gave one of the pipes a rap with his knuckles. He expected a hollow sound, but got nothing out of it.

"Who built it?" he asked, trying to appear unconcerned.

"The men," Kingsley replied.

"Which men?"

He obviously did not want to tell Henry.

"But what is it? Does it symbolise something? Is it just some piece of abstract sculpture?" Henry was teasing him. "It doesn't have a purpose, surely?"

Now, however, Kingsley was saying no more. His dumbness annoyed Henry so he kicked the pipes in front of him. They were solid and still made no sound.

"Does my father know what it is?" Henry asked.

"I promise you that I have no idea," came the quiet voice from behind Kingsley. Henry's father stood in the doorway, but the old employee did not turn to look at him. "I'm sorry, Kingsley," he said, "but this thing has been getting in the way long enough, and I can't see that it serves any purpose."

Under the light from the panels in the roof the old man's head, with its smooth white skin, looked slightly luminous, and Henry was reminded of the pallor of albino crabs that live in caves in complete darkness.

Henry walked around the object, with Kingsley following at a suspicious distance, and stopped at the control panel. Henry noticed with some satisfaction that the man was following him almost subserviently, cowed.

"Is this meant to turn it on?" Henry asked, but again Kingsley said nothing; he simply stared at Henry, almost waiting to see what he would do next.

"What happens if I flip a switch?"

Henry was annoyed by the man's lack of answers. He abruptly pulled on a lever, and when nothing happened he turned a dial and flicked a big brass switch.

"It's a fake, or a hoax," Henry said. "It doesn't do anything. It's quite impressive," he admitted, in a friendly, conversational tone, before saying, with some venom, "but it's really only so much scrap metal . . . "

None of his goading seemed to have worked. He stared at Kingsley, for the first time realising that he was actually taller than the man. Old age had shrunk the fellow, Henry realised. He wasn't the ogre he remembered. He laughed, and Kingsley said something under his breath.

"What did you say?"

"Is it really to be taken down?" Kingsley quietly asked, almost subservient.

"Yes, and this pit will have to be covered over . . . "

Guilt was creeping into Henry's heart. The pathetic old specimen in front of him was genuinely distraught. Henry looked around the gloomy building, embarrassed now, and saw his father standing several yards away, observing them.

"This thing just can't stay," he explained. "And why should it? What does it do?"

The old man said nothing; he was looking down at his boots.

"I don't believe that it has any purpose at all," Henry said, exasperated that the man was regaining his power over him; this time through his unspoken demand for sympathy.

"If it was anything other than just a vast mess of old gas pipes that might be different, but it isn't, is it?"

Kingsley looked over at Henry's father. He appeared to be about to rub that great jaw of his, perhaps in contemplation, but he had already made up his mind. Perhaps, thought Henry, there was even a smirk on his face, but he simply walked to the control panel.

"I'll show you why it must stay," he said. "And why nobody else must be told about it."

The big room was silent; no sounds came from outside; not even the noise of traffic on the main road.

Kingsley flicked the switch back off, moved the lever to its original position and changed the setting on the dial that Henry had turned. With reluctance, he pressed a button and carefully manipulated the two dials at the same time, one in either hand. His head was tilted to one side as though he was listening for something. He brought down the lever very slowly, at the same time turning the second dial back to what appeared to be its original position. He smiled to himself and pressed the switch and stood back, looking at the mass of pipes in front of him with a sense of admiration.

"There were to be eleven of these," he said, with pride. "Each numbered, and positioned."

"What number was this one?" Henry asked, unwillingly humouring him.

"This was number one. It was the first," he said looking at Henry to see if he now understood.

"Where were the others to be positioned?"

"I can only tell you so much. But, listen . . . "

Henry heard nothing and shook his head.

Kingsley's expression changed to bewilderment.

"You don't hear it?" he asked.

"Hear what?"

He took a step back to the control panel and turned the first dial slightly. When he looked at Henry once more, for confirmation that he now heard, he could only shake his head again. Kingsley turned the dial a little further, all the time watching to see if Henry's expression had changed. However, there was still no sound; the room was as quiet as before, and when Henry's father moved the noise he made only highlighted the overwhelming silence.

"The others weren't ever built," said Henry, but Kingsley didn't appear to have heard him. The man was becoming angry now, turning the dial inexorably but ineffectually around to its maximum, grimacing as he did so. He suddenly looked pleadingly at Henry, and he seemed to be in real pain. Suddenly he was impelled to clasp his hands to his ears and screamed out: "How can you stand it? How can you stand it?"

Henry was taken aback by the volume of the shouting. He looked at his father who appeared to be as surprised as he was.

"Why don't you suggest he turns it off?" he suggested to Henry from across the room.

"But that would be going along with his crazy game."

Henry looked back at Kingsley and relented, reluctantly, telling him that he should stop the demonstration. However, by then he was crouching on the floor with his arms around his head.

"Why don't you turn it off," Henry shouted at him, but still the man did not seem to hear.

"Turn it off!" he shouted again in anger and exasperation. There was nothing to be heard, but the man seemed to be in genuine distress. Feeling as though a great practical joke was being played out at his expense Henry strode to the control panel and turned the dials anti-clockwise and pushed back the lever. He flicked the switch off, but he refused to believe that it would change anything.

He turned back to Kingsley, prepared to tell him to go to hell, but the man was still crouched on the floor. Slowly, gingerly he was taking his arms from around his head, as if convinced that they would have to be replaced at any moment.

"What on earth do you think you're doing?" Henry demanded, but was ignored. "Kingsley!" he said, bending down and taking him roughly under one arm. "Explain what you think you're doing?"

Slowly the old man looked up at Henry, imploringly, and large tears were running down his smooth face.

"Kingsley?" he said, calmer now, realising that the man couldn't hear him.

Kingsley spent several weeks in hospital, and then Henry's father paid for him to stay in a convalescent home on the coast for a couple of months. Apparently the old man was described by the doctors as highly agitated and confused, but not delusional. Within a few weeks he became calm and seemed to be stable, but he remained quite deaf, and continued to suffer from terrible headaches. He moved back home, but not before Henry's father had arranged for the dismantling of the giant device in the green store. As the weather had taken a turn for the worse the company employed to take it apart were glad to do so within the building itself, so the public only ever saw lorry after lorry drive off with more and more cast iron pipe. The biggest problem that they encountered in dismantling it was when the whole thing fell into the pit at an odd angle. However, once it was wedged there the job continued without too many problems. People from the very few neighbouring businesses joked about the capacity of the building to hold so much scrap metal.

Henry's mother and father moved out from the flat above the shop and never knew whether Kingsley returned to the site of the ironmongers while the dismantling and demolition work was undertaken. They were told by friends that when the developers finally removed the green store everyone came to see the vast pit that was uncovered. Engineers made their reports and pronounced it structurally sound and unlikely to collapse so the bridge was made to span it and the whole thing was sealed off. With asphalt over the site of Kingsley's great device, the trucks that now entered the industrial complex would have no idea of what had been there before. Kingsley took his redundancy cheque and was never in contact with my father again.

The following year Henry visited his parents in their new house on the edge of the country, on the other side of town. He asked his father if anybody had taken a photo of what had been standing in the green store for all of those years, but nobody had thought to do so. When Henry reminded his father of this some years later he denied that there had ever been anything there at all. His father, though, seemed to go into a decline after he retired, and his memory started to fail, to his wife's distress. And she refused to talk about Kingsley and his construction.

Afterwards

Toby has left. I suppose that his departure was inevitable. After the people in the army vehicles had gone, he spent more and more time in the top room, staring out of the window, looking for possible visitors. This wasn't just because he agreed we should be more vigilant; he was actually wanting them to return, or for somebody else to come and see if the castle was occupied. Toby understood exactly why I wouldn't let anyone in, but, eventually, he went looking for them.

I got up at seven, as usual, to make breakfast. He had left a note, apologising for leaving the door unlocked and undefended. He had calculated his departure so that I could not follow him. He had walked down to the village, taken the small van, and had left just before the rising tide covered the causeway and cut off the island. He said he might come back, but he didn't know . . .

I secured the main door, then went up onto the roof. There was always a chance he had changed his mind, or hadn't been able to start the van, but there was nobody in sight. Up there, looking out over the battlements, the view was, as always, almost unendurably beautiful. Nothing stirred on the island below, apart from the over-wintering geese, and the whole long arc of the mainland beach was deserted. The only thing moving was a large flock of un-identifiable birds that turned in on itself and spread out over the gunmetal grey sea, fading into the distance. I took out the telescope and set it up, scanning the line of the sandy, potholed road that follows the slight ridge that used to take visitors to and from the village. I looked beyond the water that now covered the causeway, where the faint line of the road emerged briefly on the mainland before disappearing once more.

He had gone.

I first met Toby in Berwick, back when I used to travel around much more, trying to work out what to do, how to survive. I was usually very careful; I was more than just wary of meeting anyone. If I ever heard vehicles, or saw smoke in the distance, which happened occasionally, I invariably went in the other direction. But as I walked into the town that day without thinking about concealing myself, he stepped out of a doorway, levelling a shotgun at my head. It had happened to me once before, and again I was shaking with fear, but this time the weapon was in the hands of a child. He had been fifteen at the time.

"How can I help?" I asked carefully, and because he didn't say anything.

The boy looked ill. He stank. His eyes were dark-rimmed, his skin a mess, and his cheekbones were angular and ugly. He was shaking, which didn't give me any confidence that he might not be about to shoot me.

I forced myself to be calm. I swallowed. I didn't quite repeat myself; I said, "Can I help?"

"How?"

"I came into town looking for supplies."

"Can you cook me something?"

It wasn't what I expected him to say. I asked him what he liked to eat and he shrugged. I asked him to lower his gun and he did, although he kept it ever ready, suspicious. My heart continued to beat fast. I was short of breath.

"Where's worth looking for food?" I asked, trying to appear calm and friendly, unconcerned. He pointed towards a newsagent's, but I didn't hold out much hope; like most shops, the window was smashed and it had obviously been looted. The cigarettes and alcohol were all gone, as were most of the sweets, but I found some tinned meat pies at the back, hidden under old newspapers. There were also some tins of peas, beans, and peach slices. Other packet food, convenience, stuff, seemed to have spoiled. Scavenging was always hit and miss; some shops had been left completely untouched, while others had been systematically stripped of all non-perishables.

"*Where* shall I cook?" I asked, and the boy motioned with his gun that we should go out.

The house where he had been living was filled with rubbish, especially empty bottles, and it smelt as bad as he did. I cleared a surface in the kitchen, and the gas oven lit easily, once I had turned on the bottle outside. I put in the meat pie, and found pans to cook the vegetables.

"Where do you get water?" I asked, and he pointed to a plastic container. I didn't want to know where it had come from; we were going to boil it, after all.

"My name's John McGovern," I said.

It was only after we had finished eating that he finally told me his name: Toby.

The gun had been leant against the table all the time. All through the meal his eyes had darted towards it, making sure he could grab it if he needed to.

"It's nice to meet you, Toby. You're here on your own?"

"Why am I alive?" he asked. "My mum and dad are dead. And my grandparents. And all of my friends."

"There's nobody else in town?"

"People pass through, sometimes, not often, taking stuff, wrecking the place. I hide."

"That's sensible."

"But why am I still alive? Why are you?"

"We're the lucky ones."

"Are we?"

"I think so."

"Is everyone dead all over the world? I kept thinking that maybe people from the south would come up to help us; from London. Or the Americans. Or Australians—they're a long way away."

"Nobody's coming," I said, wondering if I should really be so brutal. I told him, "For a long time I could hear radio stations broadcasting from different parts of the world, but they've all gone dead now."

"So we're on our own?"

"Pretty much."

"What do we do?"

"Try and survive."

"How do you do it?"

"I've got stuff stored, and I grow vegetables. I've even got some goats, for milk. I keep out of the way of the people who are left."

"Will you take me with you?"

"I'm used to living on my own."

"*Please*."

His despair was profound. I thought he'd be disappointed when I said, "I'll see," but the sudden hope in his eyes was almost overwhelming. I hadn't been around people for over a year and I was both scared of, and yet yearned for company.

I also felt angry that he had frightened me. He had forced an acquaintance, at best, and a meal, through the use of a gun.

"It isn't loaded," he said. "I haven't got any cartridges left. I used to go around town shooting at stuff, but then I couldn't find any more ammo."

"How have *you* survived this long?"

"I take stuff from the shops. I used to just eat sweets, but I soon got sick of them. I actually got *really* sick, so I try eating other stuff. I have a cat. I've got lots of food for that. This isn't my house, you know. I can't go back home; it's horrible there. *This* house used to belong to some people called Clarke, but I think it was a holiday home. How long has it been since everybody died?"

I brought my van from where I had left it, as usual, just out of town, and I parked it close to his house. Toby helped me find what supplies I could, which were still available if you looked in the less obvious places. I even risked going inside some houses, although Toby refused to do so. When everything went wrong people invariably took to their beds, and stayed there to die. It had been a hot summer when it happened, and though it was now past the point where most houses smelt so horribly of death, you could usually see where the former owners had decayed through the ceiling from the bedrooms above.

I really considered going back to the castle without Toby. I was still annoyed that he had threatened me, although I knew that it hadn't been unreasonable in the circumstances. Toby had all kinds of health issues, and, as I soon discovered, a drink problem.

The first night, back on the island, I was nervous, convinced I had done the wrong thing by letting him return with me. I lowered the portcullis that had once been an affectation in a resolutely Arts and Crafts fortification, and I locked the massive timber door, pocketing the key rather than leaving it on the hook as I normally did. I even locked my own bedroom door, and listened for several sleepless hours to hear if Toby was moving around. He had drunk a bottle of wine by himself that evening, but it meant that he slept.

"What's going to happen?" Toby asked over breakfast the next morning. He had asked for tinned meat pie again—he insisted he had enjoyed the previous one more than any meal he could remember. He really had survived for two years on an abominable diet of packaged snacks, sweets, and alcohol.

"Long term?" I asked, and he nodded. "I don't know. I can't guess how many people are still alive. Very, very few. After the worst of it was over, I went down through Tyneside, Newcastle, Gateshead and saw people, but only a dozen, perhaps, in a city of, I don't know, a million? We could probably all survive for several lifetimes on what's left in tins and bottles and packets. But how many know how to grow fresh food? They can learn, that's what I'm doing, but there aren't enough people to keep the electric grid going, or the water supply, or the sewers.

"The only other time anybody pointed a gun at me was in Middlesbrough. The man was coming out of a shop, stealing jewellery. Gold and diamonds were rare once, but the balance of supply and demand has changed; who wants them? You can't eat metal or stones, no matter how precious."

Toby thought about this and finally said, "If people aren't alive they can't own stuff; so it's not really stealing."

I showed him around the castle. The room that fascinated him the most was my library. At first I had gone to book and antique shops finding rare and lovely things to make my new home look good and comfortable, but I soon replaced many of the antiquarian books with ones on gardening, goat husbandry, survival techniques, mending motors, nursing, handicrafts.

"We're entering a new Dark Age," Toby said, showing wisdom that surprised me. "It's like when the Romans deserted Britain; those left behind used what they could, but let everything difficult or clever fall into disrepair."

I was impressed by the way that Toby weaned himself off the alcohol. After only a few months I felt comfortable letting him lower the portcullis and lock the door at night. He approved of me not drawing attention to where we were living; I used blackout, and kept my two vans hidden in the village. Yes, the castle, on its rocky outcrop was prominent, but it couldn't be seen from the main road back on the mainland. It was once a visitor attraction, but who was left who might have the leisure to go sight-seeing?

Toby spent hours that summer in the walled vegetable garden. It was already there when I had arrived, only slightly overgrown, and it was at a discreet distance from where I actually lived. I also kept goats there, somehow, although I had problems getting them to give me any of their horrible tasting milk. Toby delighted in the creatures, though, partly because they seemed to take to him, and he became good at milking them.

It was Toby's idea to go to the mainland to find a generator. Although we never managed to wire it up to the castle's electricity supply, we used it to charge batteries and worked out how to power a TV and DVD player. I'd have liked to get the washing machine working, it really should have been possible, but we failed. Toby's enthusiasm meant that he eventually set up a computer for playing games. He admitted, later, that he had hoped to find some way of connecting to the internet. Sadly, that was never going to happen.

That summer was the first enjoyable time I had lived through since the virus. Even the winter was not so bad now that I had company. We both read a lot of biographies, watched films, and talked about what the world had been like when everybody was alive. I told Toby about my wife and children, my work, and the travelling we had done. Every morning, over breakfast, we told each other what we had dreamed about in the night. My dreams were always of friends and relatives I had once known. Toby's dreams were also full of people, but he said that he had forgotten who they might once have been.

That winter we saw a car drive into the village. Through the telescope we could make out a couple of men, and though they stayed for almost a week, they never came as far as the castle, and they left without knowing we were there. Only a few days after that, however, we were in the garden, working, and were surprised to see a man in rags looking over the wall at us. He had a long beard like old father time, but he refused to talk to us and soon walked off, muttering under his breath. Of rather more interest that winter was a very large container ship that ran aground about a mile up the coast. I was surprised that there were still any ships on the oceans that hadn't sunk or been washed-up. In the early days I used to watch them out in the North Sea, drifting aimlessly, but this ship must have been out there for nearly three years before it landed near us.

A few weeks later I was up on the roof when I saw, in the distance, an organised band of people climbing up the hull of the ship. Through the telescope I could see that there were at least twenty of them, and they had fashioned some kind of ladder. I couldn't see what they were doing once they were aboard, but they seemed to leave a few hours later without taking anything off the ship. Their vehicles disappeared out of sight for only a few minutes. I next saw them coming over the causeway.

My castle is a real one, and it is *my* castle, because, as Toby said, if there's nobody else to own something, it's yours. The castle dates back to the sixteenth century, and despite being remodelled as a house at the very beginning of the twentieth century, it would still take some storming. I had always felt secure, but I had seen that these people had ladders that could presumably reach us. Toby immediately had my shotguns and ammunition up on the roof. He was ready for a fight.

"The guns are just for show," I said to him. "We frighten them off, but we don't actually shoot anyone."

"I saw people killed when I lived in Berwick," he said. "It's them or us."

"Not necessarily. We don't know they want to attack us. Besides, there are only two of us, and there's, maybe, a couple of dozen of them."

"But we have the high ground. And we could sit out a siege for years with what we've got stored away."

"I don't want to kill anyone. And I don't want a siege."

"What are you going to do? Talk to them? Reason with them?"

"If I have to, yes. Most people are decent."

Looking back on what happened, I know that I wanted to show Toby that not all in the world was bad; not everything had been ruined by the virus. I went out to talk to our visitors while he stayed behind with the guns. If I failed, then the portcullis was ready to fall, the door to be locked.

I admit that I was scared. I could barely call down to them to ask what they wanted. Seeing I had no weapon, the two men who walked forward were also unarmed. Others, in the background, though, had guns.

"What do you want?" I shouted.

"We're travelling north, seeing what we can find as we go. We want a doctor. One of our party is sick."

"I was an accountant," I told them.

They laughed and the other man said, "What use would you be to anyone now?"

"I survive."

"We're looking for people with skills to join us. We want teachers."

"Good luck with that."

"We've got plenty of food and medicines. We don't want anything from you."

"Okay. I wish you luck."

"Good luck yourself."

They started to walk off, but I couldn't help calling after them, "Any news?"

"Of what?" asked the first man. "We're all fucked."

"Anything from abroad?"

"Nothing we know of. But it's all going wrong down south. We're off to Scotland."

"What's going wrong?"

"People, animals, birds, all getting sick and dying. We think it's the power stations, the nuclear ones. Did they manage to shut them down in time? To quarantine them? Who knows?"

Toby was so angry with me for talking to them that he didn't ask what we had discussed. Afterwards he insisted we go and get more guns, grenades, even, but the best we could find were two more shotguns in farmhouses that he refused to enter. We tried an army base; part of it was so secure that we couldn't get in, and the rest had already been emptied. I was pleased, though that we returned with some good shovels and a great number of top-quality candles. A few weeks later Toby wanted to go off the island again, to find weapons, but we ended up in a garden centre instead and brought back a flat-pack greenhouse, some fruit bushes and a lot of seeds. We saw another rag-tag convoy on the main road that time, but we kept out of their way.

We were very busy in the spring, and by early summer the vegetables were doing far better than in previous years.

Toby would go over to the mainland on his own and reported that while he did not see any vehicles, it was obvious that some had passed through. By this time the grass verges of the road had encroached so as to make previously wide stretches of tarmac into single lanes, and bushes, rampant brambles and especially overhanging trees, meant that in some places following the road was not easy.

We only had two more visitors that summer; an old couple who rambled hopelessly when we gave them a meal, but who moved on the next day. They tried to give me a Bible and, when I told them that I was not religious, the woman said that neither were they. They had been, she explained, but no longer. They hoped somebody could find comfort in it. Toby promised them he would read it, which pleased them, but I am not sure he ever did.

We were working in the garden one afternoon in August when we heard the engines. Looking over the wall we saw the army vehicles in the village and we dropped everything. We ran back across to the castle and up the ramp, and we managed to shut ourselves in just before they could reach us. We ran up to the roof and looked down over the battlements to see them below, at our door. They were hammering at it, and shouting to one another.

"You're not talking to this lot," insisted Toby, and I agreed with him. A few moments later there was the unmistakeable sound of a shotgun, and then a second blast. They hung around for over an hour, even trying to light a fire against the door, but eventually drove off. We could see lights in the village that night, and fires, and the next morning we watched them drive in convoy to the causeway, where the tide was coming up fast. Half of their vehicles got across, but the rest were stranded, and remained there, the engines waterlogged. We kept well away, and eventually they disappeared.

And then Toby left. I hadn't told him about everything "going wrong" down south. I didn't tell him that things were going wrong where we were. Although the garden looked good, I had lifted a few potatoes and carrots, and within the soil the vegetables were shrivelled and unhealthy. The goats were also beginning to look ill, and there was less milk than usual. Toby left at the right time, or perhaps he should have left a little earlier. I don't know. But I'm not going anywhere.

Most days I go up on the roof with the telescope, but I don't see any people or vehicles. I watch a lot of films, and play Toby's computer games. When I dream, I no longer remember the names of the people I still recognise from my past. It is autumn, and I am expecting the geese to return, but they are late this year.

The Ghosts of Begbie Hall

"**M**rs. Taylor?"

The greeting came from a woman sitting in a ponderous wingback chair by the front door. Because of the paperwork on her lap she could not immediately stand.

"I'm Mrs. Reynolds," she said.

Sarah Taylor walked over, leaving the hotel receptionist to wait patiently.

"I'm so pleased you finally agreed to come to one of our little conferences," Mrs. Reynolds cooed.

Sarah could not reply to that. Over the last ten years she had declined Mrs. Reynolds' invitation three times. She was not quite sure why she had finally accepted.

"Begbie Hall has changed," said Mrs. Reynolds. She was able to stand once she had heaped the papers untidily on to the floor.

"I knew the Hall when it was occupied by the Walker family," Sarah said.

"We're familiar with your father's first book. Then there was the fire, of course, and for several years this place was falling down . . . "

"I know the history."

"Of course. And you have written your 'talk' for us?"

"I have."

Mrs. Reynolds insisted they shake hands rather formally, and she allowed Sarah to return to the reception desk. She signed the register and was given an electronic key card.

"You are in the Red Room," said the receptionist.

For the first time since she had pulled up at Begbie Hall, a slight thrill coursed through Sarah.

"Do you still call it 'The Red Room'?"

Mrs. Reynolds explained: "When our conference isn't on, when ghost hunters *aren't* here, it's called the 'Lady Caroline Room'; goodness only knows why. The name-plate on the door is changed for us. It's not a problem, is it?" she asked. And then added what sounded like a statement, rather than another question: "I mean, you don't believe in the ghosts of Begbie Hall, do you?"

"No, I don't believe in ghosts, but that doesn't mean I'm not scared of them."

Mrs. Reynolds nodded and acknowledged the source of the quote, "Madame du Deffand". She said to Sarah: "I can always have your room changed. There are guests in the new annexe who'd give their eye-teeth to stay in The Red Room."

"No, that won't be necessary. If I remember rightly, it has lovely views over the countryside. If I find myself spooked, then I'll tell myself I'm in the 'Lady Caroline Room'."

No *frisson* went through Sarah as she entered the Red Room for the first time in thirty-five years. The Hall had always lacked character; it was "foursquare" and plain, an expansive Victorian version of Georgian. The main rooms were all unadorned, high-ceilinged, and with large-paned sash windows. The abstract art now on the white walls did not contribute to any kind of atmosphere. The furniture was modern and of good quality; most guests would consider the room bright and comfortable. The Hall had been renovated and converted into a hotel, she assumed, because it offered so much accommodation beyond the main reception rooms and seven bedrooms, what with the sculleries, wash-rooms, stables, etc. Permission had been granted for the development of an annexe at the back where a number of barns had once stood, although Sarah could not remember the original buildings being quite as extensive as the replacements. Begbie Hall was convenient for the Norfolk Broads and not too distant from some tolerable main roads. Its history as a haunted house simply added the opportunity for the management to rent out a few more rooms to ghost-hunters in the off-season.

Sarah Taylor looked out of the bedroom window and for a fraction of a second was confused. She had expected, momentarily, to see the view as she had last witnessed it, when she had seen Terrence Walker. Then it had been a hot summer afternoon and there had been beds of vibrant foxgloves on either side of a large lawn which led down to the pond. All that Sarah could see now, peering into the foggy autumn day, looked dull and formal. The visibility was even worse than when she had left David and the two children in Lancaster that morning. She had been forced to drive carefully, slowly, all the way to Begbie Hall, but she had been happy to take her time, and to put off her arrival. She had even made a diversion to Fairhurst on the way, to look at the river, and to remember Terrence.

Sarah thought about the talk that she was to give that evening. David had helped compose her half-dozen pages of reminiscences and to put them into some semblance of order, but he had been unable to make her explain her motivation in going back to the Hall, to finally talk to the ghost hunters.

"I'll leave you to unpack and freshen up," said Mrs. Reynolds, surprising Sarah that she was still there, standing in the doorway. "Perhaps we can meet for a drink in the old drawing room at six?"

Sarah decided not to unpack her bag, but to take out of it anything she might require only as and when it was needed. She didn't want to "freshen up", either; to put off her arrival she had not long since stopped at a service station where she had taken her time over a coffee and had used their toilet.

She unearthed her "talk" from the bag, along with the original edition of her father's first book, *The Ghosts of Begbie Hall*. Then she opened the zipped pocket on the side of the bag and took out ten small pebbles that she slipped into her right trouser pocket.

Sarah opened the book at the plan of the first floor of the Hall, and compared the dimensions of the original Red Room to the one in which she now stood. She had known that it was different the moment she had entered; there had once been a small dressing room which was now the *en suite* bathroom, and both rooms had been slightly remodelled. In the bathroom itself the window had been moved from the east wall to the west.

She made sure that she had the key card, and went out into the hallway. As far as she could tell that was unchanged from the original layout. The room opposite, once the Yellow Room, Terrence Walker's bedroom, was another guest bedroom, although there was now a second door at the end of the corridor. As that had no name plate she assumed that it was probably a new cupboard or storeroom.

As she walked back to the stairs she passed the position of what her father had insisted on calling the "cold spot", but she felt nothing; the hotel central heating was, if anything, a little stifling. The chandelier over the stairwell was resolutely modern, and all around her the panelling was of some light wood and obviously new. It was here that the ghost of the old man was meant to have been seen, but Sarah could not believe that any self-respecting member of the spirit world would now want to haunt Begbie Hall.

Down the long second corridor there were five more bedrooms where there would originally have only been four. She was sad to see that the narrow back stair had been removed and replaced by a lift; she would be mentioning the second staircase in her "talk". There was then a fire door leading out to the annexe at the back. It was almost impossible to believe that this was the same house that the Walkers had once lived in, or the derelict building that her father had so carefully continued to investigate for spirits.

Sarah ventured downstairs. It was deserted and she was pleased to meet no other guests or any members of staff. Off the hallway, the two main reception rooms were almost unchanged from how she remembered them, apart from the décor and furnishings, and the addition of a small bar in the old drawing room. The study appeared to be the hotel office, and several other rooms had all been found new uses; one was even fitted-out with a computer for the use of guests.

The corridor to the new annexe also led to the dining room which was in the old courtyard, now covered with a glazed roof. There were small palm trees in pots, and on the floor there were new flagstones rather than the bricks that had once paved the area.

"Mrs. Taylor," exclaimed Mrs. Reynolds from behind her once again. This time Sarah turned to see the woman with two men whom she judged to be older than she was. Introductions were made, and the two eager members of the society both insisted that they buy her a drink.

"This is slightly awkward," Sarah admitted as she sat with a gin and tonic in one hand, and her father's book in the other. After only fifteen minutes she was the centre of attention for a dozen members of the society. "I hope to answer all of your questions in the talk I'm giving tonight."

"No spoilers!" declared a man in a cravat.

A tall woman with her hair in an elaborate pile on her head said, "We look forward to it," but Mrs. Reynolds talked over her as though she was not present:

"Perhaps we should tell you all about *ourselves*."

There was general approval for the idea, and the president of the society was the first to compose herself and begin.

"I founded the Begbie Hall Society in 1984. I had only just moved into the old blacksmith's cottage in the village. One of my neighbours lent me your father's first book. Of course, I immediately came down to the Hall to take a look. At that time the builders were at work in earnest—it was a construction site. There was no roof, and some of the walls were down. The garden was just an acre of mud and machinery. The site foreman showed me around, and explained what they were doing, and I asked him if he had noticed anything strange about the Hall. He said that he hadn't; he was a big, no-nonsense kind of man, a hard-headed northerner, but apparently one of his builders had claimed that, a few times, when he had been inside the shell of the Hall, he had been convinced that somebody had called to him from outside. When he had gone to see who it was, nobody was there. His workmates said it wasn't them and, besides, he said he thought it had been a woman's voice.

"I went back many times," said Mrs. Reynolds, "and they said that nothing else had been experienced, apart from the theft of some materials. But, of course, they were never at the Hall at night. Although it's almost a mile from the village, I used to walk my dog down here in the evenings and it was always very eerie. There was nothing specific, but I've always been sensitive, and I knew that the real inhabitants of the Hall were disturbed by what was going on . . .

"When it was eventually opened as a hotel I got to know the first manager, Mr. Pinfold, and he had no interest in the history of the building whatsoever. He wanted nothing to do with ghosts. I told him it could be a tourist attraction, but he was of the opinion that such stories would put-off guests rather than attract them. I started the Begbie Hall Society in spite of Pinfold. I'd book the Red Room and the old drawing room, and a few friends would come along to stay. We would hold séances. The management disapproved; Pinfold even tried throwing us out one time, but one of our party was a solicitor and threatened him with legal action. Anyway, I wrote my own book about our findings. I interviewed the staff, other guests . . . "

"This one!" said a woman in a cardigan with a repeated design of cats over it. She waved before her a cheap paperback with a lurid cover.

"Thank you, Zara. Well, Mrs. Clarke was the manager after Mr. Pinfold, and she was no more sympathetic. But when Eastern Hotels bought the Hall ten years ago their manager, Mr. Pardew, encouraged our society. He even put up photos of the old Hall, and allowed us to leave leaflets about the ghosts. My book and a reprint of your father's book used to be for sale at the reception desk. When we held our conferences they were happy to change the names of the rooms for us. For several years the conferences were so well attended that we booked-out the whole hotel for long weekends. We had ghosts-hunts throughout the night. All the best cutting-edge scientific equipment was brought here by some very eminent scientists, and we occasionally had startling results. You'll have seen the articles in the *Telegraph* and *Mail* about five years ago?

"For the last three years the attendance has been down and we've had to share our weekends with other guests. We try not to disturb them, although last year one woman we met was sure that she had also seen a grey figure on the long corridor, and in broad daylight too!"

After Mrs. Reynolds had spoken, a Mr. Brown, vice chairman of the society, talked about his scientific training and his experiences of various haunted houses, both in England and America. They proudly discussed a Mrs. Trivet, who was a well-respected medium, now too elderly to attend the conferences. Her results in contacting the Chapman family, who had first built Begbie Hall in 1870, were, apparently, remarkable. And then there was Mr. Durrant who was obsessed by the photos he had taken in the Hall with a particular camera that captured "orbs", whatever they were. It sounded to Sarah as though the man's camera was probably faulty.

She listened to stories that were all told with an assurance that suggested they were often repeated. From the moment she walked into the old drawing room a resentment had started to rise up in her, along with a nervousness that she tried to ignore. She ran her fingers through the smooth pebbles in her pocket and felt tempted to throw them at the self-satisfied and excitable members of the society who were paying her expenses. It seemed obvious that Mr. Brown was a fraud, the cat-cardigan lady was a needy type, the man with a cravat a small-time crook, and Mr. Durrant simple-minded, while Mrs. Reynolds . . . well she was harder to pin down, but Sarah could imagine that if she had moved to any other village she might have started a society to keep green the memory of a local poet, or to force open footpaths blocked by farmers. She was that type . . .

Dinner was, frankly, hard work. Sarah had Mrs. Reynolds to one side of her and Mr. Durrant the other. A young couple faced them, Americans, and their enthusiasm for Begbie Hall seemed to drain away any that Sarah might have had herself. She was becoming increasingly concerned that her talk was not well-considered. She wondered why she had written it; these people were tiresome, but she had to admit to herself that they were essentially harmless. Why did she want to spoil their weekend? Why, when all they were doing was escaping from monotonous lives to spend the weekend looking for ghosts?

After dinner there was a half hour before she was expected to address the society, and Sarah went up to her room and wasted most of her time looking for her "talk", which she was sure she had taken out of her bag earlier. She was not certain she could say anything to them without it, although she might be able to get David to find it on their home computer and email it to the hotel to print another copy.

But just as she was certain she would have to call her husband, she opened the bedside drawer and there were the printed sheets. Too relieved to wonder why, she then realised that she had misplaced her copy of her father's book.

The book was down in the drawing room, where she had left it earlier.

"Mrs. Sarah Taylor," announced Mrs. Reynolds, "is the daughter of the late Jeremy Taylor, author of *The Ghosts of Begbie Hall*, and the sequel volume, *Further Ghosts of Begbie Hall*. Sarah Taylor is the child mentioned in chapter two as having talked to a 'strange lady' in the long corridor on the first floor. We have invited her to speak to our society several times, but she has always declined with a polite note saying that she doesn't believe in ghosts. Be that as it may, she has kindly consented to come and talk to us this evening."

There was polite applause, and Sarah made her way into the corner where she stood dutifully behind a low lectern. She laid out her sheets of paper, looked up, and almost froze.

"Thank you, um, thank you, Mrs. Reynolds."

She looked down at the words that seemed suddenly indistinct. Her audience patiently waited for her to change her glasses, but the height of the lectern meant that she was expected to focus somewhere between the ideal distance for either set of spectacles. She lifted the pages and the first words became readable. She grasped at them.

"I was born in Fordbury," she said. "Just up the road. And I lived there with my mother and father until I went to secondary school in 1970. Then we moved to Begbie village, two doors up from the blacksmith's, where Mrs. Reynolds now lives. My father, Jeremy Taylor was a decorator, and my mother, Lily, a scientist. Until my father became interested in ghosts he had been an amateur water-colourist, and at one time a fisherman. He also tried woodcarving, lino-cutting, basket-weaving, and he was rather good at indoor bowls. My mother called him a gadfly, always flitting from one interest to another. She, as I said, was a scientist, although I use the term without quite understanding what she did. She started off as a laboratory assistant for ICI, but then worked in a research department which grew strains of pest-resistant wheat.

"I tell you all of this because it's right that you should have some background. In my father's books he doesn't say very much about himself, or his family. One of the things he should have mentioned was that I was the one who introduced him to the Walkers of Begbie Hall. You see, Terrence Walker was a friend and we travelled into school together on the bus every day. A lot of people thought we were boyfriend and girlfriend, but we weren't. We did see a lot of each other, but it was mainly through proximity.

"I was the first of my family to visit Begbie Hall. The story of me having talked to a 'strange lady' on the first floor is one that I really don't remember. It was something my father resurrected when I told him the story of the very first odd thing that I distinctly recall having happened here. I'd been coming to the Hall for a couple of years, and I remember clearly that it was tea time, and in the corner of the kitchen, where nobody was standing, a cup seemed to lift itself up off the table and fall to the floor, where it smashed. I don't remember it as being at all frightening or spooky—it was simply very odd. Mr. Walker was annoyed, but Terrence suddenly got angry. His mother was, like me, bemused. But, later on, other things happened. On another visit a light bulb exploded, and on a later occasion a basket full of washing fell down the stairs of its own volition. And Terrence said he had seen an old man in the corridor one morning as he was coming down to breakfast.

"I thought it was all a lot of nonsense, and I told my father so. I remember that we had a discussion with my mother about poltergeists, and she explained that there was well-recorded evidence of the phenomena. Apparently poltergeists were associated with troubled teenage girls, but she said it was probably just as true of boys. She said Terrence was highly-strung, which I thought, at the time, was a whole lot of nonsense. But I remember the conversation because it was the only time I remember my mother being at all tolerant of the supernatural; she talked about the untapped power of the human brain, telekinesis, and other phenomena. Now, if I was interested in this, I soon realised that my father was *fascinated*. As I said, it was through me that he had his first introduction to Begbie Hall, and it was the start of an enthusiasm that lasted far longer than his painting, fishing or bowls."

Sarah Taylor took a sip of water from the conveniently placed glass, and was reassured that her audience were still with her.

"Our home soon filled up with books on ghosts, hauntings, poltergeists, spirits, all kinds of esoteric, left-field and frankly loony stuff . . . My mother became more and more annoyed. I remember her lecturing my father on scientific method, and she became especially exasperated by his fondness for books on mediumship, spiritualism, and the like.

"He *did* take much of what she said to heart. He bought and borrowed equipment to measure temperature, electromagnetic fields, etc. The Walkers indulged him. I was embarrassed. And Terrence, well, I'll tell you about Terrence later . . .

"I left for college in 1977, to study geography, in Lampeter, Wales. My parents moved to Ipswich because of my mother's job. Apparently my father drove up to Begbie Hall most weekends, and I used to wonder why the Walkers put up with him. But he and Tony Walker were, by then, firm friends. They were both cricket fans and they shared a taste for vintage port. They were both a pair of old reactionaries as well. I never shared my father's politics . . .

"It was three years later that I happened to be in the area with a boyfriend, Gwilym. We were meant to have been doing some surveying up at The Wash, as a part of our college course, staying in Hunstanton. We were mainly interested in each other at the time—it was a short-lived affair. Anyway, his car started to play up and well, it was a long drive ahead of us, and Begbie village wasn't too far off. I remembered Neil Bartlett's garage, and persuaded Gwil to take the car there. Neil took a look at it and saw what was wrong, ordered a new part over the phone and promised us it would be delivered within the hour. We'd be 'good to go' some time after two . . . Gwil decided to visit the church because he was a bit of an antiquary, but I decided to wander down to Begbie Hall because, well, I'd been in the church often enough and it held no interest for me.

"When I knocked at the Hall, Terrence answered the door. His parents were away and he had the place to himself. I remember it as an idyllic afternoon . . . "

Sarah halted, remembering the sound of the insects and all the brightly-coloured foxgloves. And she remembered Terrence taking her hand.

"It was hot, and I sat in a deckchair out on the terrace. Terrence made me a glass of tonic water with ice . . . "

And she had wanted him to kiss her. How much would have changed if he had done so? She would have been willing to let him. She would have reciprocated.

"We talked," Sarah resumed, once more. "It was inevitable that we would discuss my father and the ghosts, and this, dear members of the Begbie Hall Society, is where I drop my bombshell . . . Terrence admitted that he had been responsible for *all* of the ghostly phenomena. And it wasn't because of adolescent angst and the untapped power of the human mind. He confessed that he had done it out of boredom at first. Later he took advantage of my father's enthusiasm purely for fun—it was nothing but a bit of mischief. And he wanted to apologise."

At this point in her talk Sarah Taylor put her hand in her right trouser pocket but it was empty. She patted her left pocket and found the pebbles there, which was odd. She took one out and tossed it into the lap of Mrs. Reynolds.

"You all know about the mysterious pebbles that rained down on my father in the hallway in broad daylight? Well, these are the pebbles."

She tossed another over to Mr. Durrant, who looked bemused. The lady in the cat cardigan received hers with alarm; she was the first to fully realise what Sarah had thrown and she recoiled from it with a shriek. Sarah would have thrown one to the man in the cravat, but he didn't seem to be there. Instead, she threw it to the lady with her hair piled on top of her head. Sarah smiled when she realised that the hair looked like a loaf of bread. The woman was standing at the back of the room and to Sarah's surprise she caught it very dextrously with one hand, and grinned.

"My father said in his books that the pebbles were not local to this area. He had a geologist examine them and he was told that they would have had to be imported from quite some distance. So what were they doing falling from thin air in Begbie Hall? Well, Terrence explained that they came from the river near Fairhurst, where his aunt lived. When he had visited her he brought back a box of them thinking that he would put them in the bottom of a fish tank he had; they look lovely in water. But before he had a chance to do that, my father visited, and on a whim Terrence threw them all over the banister. Apparently they made a terrible sound as they crashed onto the floor of the hallway. He ran down the back stairs, out of the side door, and he was then observed, moments later, walking nonchalantly in through the front door, asking what the fuss was all about.

Sarah Taylor's audience was silent.

"The shouts and cries from empty parts of the Hall were just as easily faked by the use of the back stairs. But anyway, calling out from one room, it was never quite possible to tell where a voice had come from. It was all a series of remarkably simple tricks. The cold spots, for example, could be arranged by leaving windows open and closing them again before my father went into a room.

By now Sarah noticed the shifting in chairs, glances between members of her audience, and even some muttering, but that was no more than she had expected.

"Chance often meant that ordinary but odd things happened and were interpreted through the pleasingly distorted prism of the supernatural. There was nothing in my father's first book that couldn't be accounted for by Terrence. And the popping light bulbs were caused by problems with the wiring which regularly blew fuses and probably accounted for the fire a year later. Luckily nobody was hurt in that."

"What about the phenomena in your father's second book?" asked a disgruntled Mr. Durrant.

"Wishful thinking," Sarah replied. "Looking at the photos he reproduced, it's obvious that the fire wasn't catastrophic. The Walkers had to move out, of course, and then there were insurance problems. Within a couple of years it was derelict. In that state my father had the run of the place along with the local foxes and owls. He continued to take his photos, and set up his experiments, but it tried my mother almost beyond the limits of endurance. When he published *The Ghosts of Begbie Hall* she was, well, mortified. When he published *Further Ghosts of Begbie Hall* she divorced him."

"Why didn't you tell your father it was all trickery?" asked another. "Before he published his second book."

"I did, but he didn't want to know."

"Mrs. Taylor," another voice came out from her audience. It took Sarah a moment to discover who had addressed her; it wasn't anybody she had seen before, over drinks or dinner.

"Mrs. Taylor," repeated a man who looked like a retired rugby player. "When did you say you visited Begbie Hall, and heard from Terrence Walker that it was all just tricks?"

"In the summer of 1980."

"But the Hall burnt down Christmas 1979," he said.

"My mistake. I must have visited in the summer of 1979. I remember that it burnt down a few months later."

"You may think we all believe in mumbo jumbo," said the man, "but we like to get our facts right. Are you sure it was 1979? You went to university when? How old are you now? If you were eighteen when you left home . . . "

Sarah interrupted: "You think that the Terrence Walker I talked to was a ghost himself?"

"And also, perhaps, the Hall itself . . . " said Mr. Durrant. "You said it appeared to you as it would have done *before* the fire. It wouldn't be the first time I've heard such a story. In Devon back in the 1950s . . . "

"I visited in '79," said Sarah firmly. "The Hall burnt down in '80, but Terrence Walker didn't die until April '84. I went to the funeral and the memorial services."

"Do you doubt the experiences of Dr. Fairbright?" asked the man obsessed by "orbs". "Or Sir Derek Biddlecomb? Major Henty or Lady Brightweather? They have all experienced just the same sort of phenomena as your father did and they are all people of the very best character."

" 'Brightweather', 'Biddlecomb', and 'Henty'?," asked Sarah, amazed and amused.

"Do you consider *your father* an intentional liar?" asked somebody else.

Mrs. Reynolds stood up and addressed the room.

"I would like to thank Mrs. Taylor for coming all the way here to talk to us today. She may not believe in ghosts, but . . . when she realises that she died in her room earlier this afternoon she will reconsider her opinion! Especially when she discovers herself destined to have to repeat her talk to us every night, forever."

Sarah knew that the laughter was very much at her expense, but it broke the awkward atmosphere, and Mrs. Reynolds was friendly when she turned and thanked her again. The man in the cravat reappeared and said that he was interested in Terrence Walker's story, and the Americans asked to have their photo taken with Sarah. She was able to slip away, though, off to her room, after only ten minutes, and she was determined to stay there. She drank the vodka from the minibar, and got out half way through soaking in the bath to find the miniature whisky and brandy bottles. It was only half past nine when she went to bed. She was determined to get up early and leave; breakfast was apparently served from seven.

Sarah awoke with a start, knowing that something was very wrong. Moving to look at the clock the whole bed seemed to move—to shift and tilt. She felt sick—it was as though she were in water, and every drop was deathly cold against her skin. All around her liquid seemed to hiss as she reached out in fear for the bedside lamp, missing the switch as the whole world seemed to rearrange itself under her. She lunged again at the light, this time turning it on, and was appalled at what she could see. Piled over the bed, and flowing on to the floor all around it, were hundreds, no, thousands of smooth, black, wet pebbles.

And the coldness from having slept on, or even in, the pebbles had entered her bones, and made it almost impossible for her to haul herself off the bed. Only once she was finally standing against the back of the bedroom door, did she realise that her nightdress was soaking. The bare skin on her arms and legs was marked by the pebbles, indented and dappled and wet, blue with the cold. She had to walk painfully over the pebbles to get into the bathroom to put on the complimentary dressing gown. Looking back into the bedroom she expected to see the illusion of the pebbles had disappeared, but they were still there, every one in the vast pile reflecting, wetly, the light of the bedside lamp. The shiver that overcame her was so profound that it almost made her fall.

And still the illusion refused to subside. After a minute her composure was not yet restored, but she was able to notice that in every other respect the room was unchanged; the chair and table, the chest of drawers, the pictures on the walls. It could only be a practical joke played upon her by the disgruntled members of the society. But how had they managed to get hold of so many pebbles, and so late on a Saturday night? They looked to be exactly the same as those she had collected on her detour to Fairhurst, but that was twenty miles away.

They would have had to gather them in the dark, and then put them in her room without her waking . . .

Sarah closed her eyes and thought. She did not want to confront anyone from the society—especially not Mrs. Reynolds. But what if it was not their work? How would she sound accusing them?

Sarah found her clothes under a layer of pebbles, where she had let them fall on the floor the night before. They were damp and creased. When she was dressed, still cold and uncomfortable, she pulled her bag out from under the stones by the bed, and she left her room, noticing how much warmer it was in the corridor. She was as quiet as possible on the stairs, and down in reception she simply left the keycard on the desk.

As she walked to the front door a voice came from the lounge:

"Mrs. Taylor?"

Sarah turned to acknowledge the greeting, even though she wanted to break into a run. She had been called by the lady in the cat cardigan, who was sitting in the semi-darkness with the man with camera that captured images of orbs. Before them, on a low table, were pieces of electrical and recording equipment, their little dials and displays glowing a variety of muted colours.

"Are you up early?" asked the woman brightly. "Or moving around the hotel rather late?"

"Early," said Sarah. "I have to leave. I've a long drive back to Lancaster."

"Well," said the man, nodding toward the equipment, "You're missing nothing here—there's been no activity at all."

"Well, goodbye," said Sarah, stopping herself from saying anything like, "It was nice to meet you."

To her relief the front door was open, and there were ineffectual lights like glow worms picking out the edge of the path to the car park. She located her car by instinct, unlocked it and threw her bag across into the passenger seat. She half expected somebody to come after her, or for the car not to start, but moments later she was driving up the lane to the village, her headlights tunnelling through the darkness.

"You're home early," said Jeremy, meeting Sarah in the hallway in his pyjamas. Their two children ran past, into the kitchen, shouting "Hi, mum!"

"I couldn't sleep," she lied. "You know what hotel rooms are like. I thought I'd drive back while there was nobody on the roads."

"So, how did it go?"

"It was a disaster," she said. "They didn't want to hear the truth—that Terrence was responsible for the ghosts of Begbie Hall. Stupid, stupid Terrence Walker."

"Poor, mixed-up Terrence," her husband corrected her. "You said he killed himself."

"Over me," she said.

Jeremy took a second to assimilate this.

"You never told me that."

"Well, no."

"You said he never left a suicide note. Nobody knew why he'd done it . . . "

"His mother did. She had a real go at me at the funeral."

"I had no idea," said her husband. He took a step forward to put his arms around Sarah, but she was hugging her overnight bag. He took it from her but could hardly bear its weight.

"Crikey, Sarah," he said. "What have you got in here?"

She frowned as he dropped the bag to the floor, at which moment a seam split down the side and dozens of shiny wet, black pebbles flowed out, clanking against each other and spreading out over the carpet.

Sources

The author would like to thank Meggan Kehrli,
Ken Mackenzie, Jim Rockhill, and Brian J. Showers for
their assistance in assembling this volume.

"Night Porter"
was first published in *Shadows & Tall Trees*,
edited by Michael Kelly, Undertow Publications, 2014.

"At the End of the World"
was first published in *Shadow's Edge*,
edited by Simon Strantzas, Gray Friar Press, 2013.

"Brighthelmstone"
was first published in *Terror Tales of the Seaside*,
edited by Paul Finch, Gray Friar Press, 2013.

"The Mighty Mr. Godbolt"
was first published in *Uncertainties II*,
edited by Brian J. Showers, Swan River Press, 2016.

"Death Makes Strangers of Us All",
"The Man Who Missed the Party", "It's Over",
"One Man's Wisdom", "Afterwards",
and "The Ghosts of Begbie Hall"
are original to this publication.

About the Author

R. B. Russell co-runs independent UK publisher Tartarus Press with Rosalie Parker. Ray's fiction has been published in four short story collections, three novellas and three novels. He has also published a biography of Robert Aickman, and a bibliographical memoir, *Fifty Forgotten Books*. Based in the Yorkshire Dales since 2000, Ray and Rosalie have a grown-up son, Tim.

SWAN RIVER PRESS

Founded in 2003, Swan River Press is an independent publishing company, based in Dublin, Ireland, dedicated to gothic, supernatural, and fantastic literature. We specialise in limited edition hardbacks, publishing fiction from around the world with an emphasis on Ireland's contributions to the genre.

www.swanriverpress.ie

"While small publishers often produce beautiful books, few can match those from Swan River Press."

– Washington Post

"It [is] often down to small, independent, specialist presses to keep the candle of horror fiction flickering . . . "

– The Irish Times

"Swan River Press—cutting edge of New Gothic."

– Joyce Carol Oates

"The redoubtable Brian J. Showers [keeps] the myriad voices of Irish fantasy alive there in Dublin."

– Alan Moore

GHOSTS

R. B. Russell

Ghosts contains R. B. Russell's debut publications, *Putting the Pieces in Place* and *Bloody Baudelaire*. Enigmatic and enticing, they combine a respect for the great tradition of supernatural fiction, with a chilling contemporary European resonance. With original and compelling narratives, Russell's stories offer the reader insights into the more hidden, often puzzling, impulses of human nature, with all its uncertainty and intrigue. There are few conventional shocks or horrors on display, but you are likely to come away with the feeling that there has been a subtle and unsettling shift in your understanding of the way things are. This book is a disquieting journey through twilight regions of love, loss, memory and ghosts. This volume contains "In Hiding", which was shortlisted for the 2010 World Fantasy Awards.

> *"Russell's stories are captivating for their depth of mystery and haunting melancholy."*

– Thomas Ligotti

> *"Russell deals in possibilities beyond the rational."*

– Rue Morgue

> *"Quiet horror told in an unassuming, polished narrative style."*

– Hellnotes

THE DARK RETURN OF TIME

R. B. Russell

*"I was searching for The Dark Return of Time on the 'net.
It's odd, but there isn't a copy for sale anywhere, and
it doesn't turn up on the British Library catalogue, the
Library of Congress website, or the Biblioteque Nationale."*

The past doesn't always stay where it should. It is as though somebody, or something, is forever trying to bring it painfully into the present.

Flavian Bennett is trying to leave his past behind when he goes to work in his father's bookshop in Paris. But a curious customer, Reginald Hopper, is desperate to resurrect his own murky origins. Hopper believes that a rare and mysterious book, The Dark Return of Time, may be the key to what happened before he arrived in Paris. In this quiet thriller by R. B. Russell, the futures—and pasts—of these two men will soon cross.

"A beautifully written and very clever work of art."

– Black Static

*"R. B. Russell's The Dark Return of Time . . .
is a short thriller that opens in a shop selling
second-hand books in Paris. What could be better?"*

– Michael Dirda, *Washington Post*

SPARKS FROM THE FIRE

Rosalie Parker

The stories in *Sparks from the Fire* explore a wide variety of familiar characters and settings, yet there is always something else—a shadow world that haunts, disturbs, and threatens. Sons and daughters, mothers and fathers, recluses and lovers—all find themselves shifting between realities: the prosaic and the mystical, even between life and death. The horrors and wonders of these parallel existences are often glimpsed, sometimes revealed, and occasionally overwhelm. These nineteen tales inhabit a terrain in which the uncanny may at any time intrude into everyday life.

"[Parker's] treatment of the fantastic is often so light and ambiguous that stories in which it does manifest are of a piece with tales such as 'Jetsam' and 'Job Start', sensitive character sketches whose celebration of life's unforeseen surprises will appeal to fantasy fans as much as the book's more overtly uncanny tales. Parker proves herself a subtle and versatile writer."

– Publishers Weekly

"If you prefer spending dark evenings with a single author, consider . . . Rosalie Parker's Sparks From the Fire, *which collects nineteen stories, some set against the brooding Yorkshire landscape."*

– Michael Dirda, *Washington Post*